THE SCOTS NEVER FORGET

You are mine!" Torquil said fiercely. "Mine, and nothing in the world will stop me from loving you and keeping you with me from now throughout eternity!"

"I . . . love . . . you!" Pepita whispered.

He would have kissed her again but she put up her hands.

"Please darling, please . . . do not make me love you any more. It . . . frightens me not because I am afraid . . . but because it is so . . . perfect . . . so wonderful!"

As if he understood he took her hands in his and raised them one after the other to his lips. As he did so Pepita realis̶ ̶ ̶ ̶ ̶ ̶ ̶ ̶ ̶ ̶ ̶ ̶ ̶ ̶ ten-sity of her feeli̶

"I adore you," ̶ ̶ ̶ ̶ ̶ ̶ ̶ ̶ ̶ ̶ ̶ g to think of you r̶ ̶ ̶ ̶ ̶ ̶ ̶ ̶ ̶ ̶ you back, but some ̶ ̶ ̶ ̶ ̶ ̶ ̶ ̶ ̶ ̶ ion to this damned mess, as quickly as possible!"

The determination in the way he spoke was inescapable and she knew, although it seemed impossible, that because he was who he was and because love was greater than anything else, that he would find a way. . . .

The Scots
Never Forget

Barbara Cartland

The Scots Never Forget

First Published in United States 1984
ⓒ 1984 Barbara Cartland
This Edition Published by **Book Essentials South** 1999
Distributed by **BMI**, Ivyland, PA 18974
PRINTED IN THE UNITED STATES OF AMERICA
ISBN 1-57723-421-9

Author's Note

The first time I visited the Highlands of Scotland, in 1927, I went to the Kirk on Sunday. It was a bleak, bare building and the Minister wore no suplice but a black cassock.

He preached a sermon which lasted for over an hour, in which he declared violently against the iniquities of the Clearances which had begun on the Glengarry Estates and had spread all over the Highlands.

He spoke so vehemently and with such intense feelings about what had occurred that I thought such terrible cruelties had just taken place. Only when I discovered that the Clearances had started in 1785 and ended in 1854 did I realise that the Scots never forget or forgive.

Heraldry arose in feudal Western Europe in the Fourteenth Century because heraldry made it possible to identify Nobles in the field of battle, and the arms became associated with heroic deeds.

The College of Arms in England dates from 1555. In Scotland the Lord Lyon is a great Officer of State, the superior Officer of Honour, and *Conseiller du Roi* in all matters armorial, genealogical, and ceremonial.

The Lord Lyon has within his power everything that appertains to the Chiefship of name and arms. The duty of this Court, which is always in session, is to establish rights to arms and pedigrees.

Chapter One

1884

*P*epita Linford walked into the Sitting-Room and looked at the packing-cases in the centre of the room, the rolled-up carpet, and the paintings which had been taken down and stacked against the walls.

There was something so depressing about it that, almost as if she winced away from what she was seeing and thinking, she walked to the window to look out at the garden.

There was still a good display of roses, dahlias, and gladioli, despite the fact that it was the beginning of September.

Beyond the garden was rolling empty land and beyond that was the sea.

She could see the blue of the Atlantic, almost as vivid as that of the Mediterranean, and knew the waves would be crashing beneath the cliffs as if they sought to destroy them.

The thought of the sea made her remember all too

1

vividly what it had taken from her, and she fought back the tears with what was a valiant effort at self-control.

As she did so she heard a knock on the front door and went across the small Hall to open it.

As she expected, a grey-haired, short, neatly dressed man was standing outside, and he smiled at the sight of her.

"Good-afternoon, Miss Linford!"

"I was expecting you, Mr. Clarence," she answered. "Will you please come in? I am afraid the only chairs we have to sit on are those in the Dining-Room."

He followed her into the small square room facing the front of the house which Lord Alistair McNairn and his wife had used as a Dining-Room.

Like the Sitting-Room, it had now been dismantled, and only a few upright leather-seated chairs remained unpacked.

Pepita sat down on one of them, and as Mr. Clarence took another she looked at him with large eyes wide and apprehensive, as if she knew already what he was going to tell her.

He moved another chair near to his, put on it a leather briefcase he had been carrying in his hand, and opened it.

"I am afraid, Miss Linford," he said as he did so, "that I do not have good news for you."

"I expected that, Mr. Clarence!"

Mr. Clarence drew from his case a sheet of foolscap paper.

He stared at it for some moments as if either what he read surprised him or he was thinking how he could explain to the girl waiting.

Then he cleared his throat, and as if he forced himself to begin he said:

"I have received the sum of three hundred twenty-two pounds from the purchasers of the horses and the furniture."

Pepita gave a little gasp.

"Is that all?"

"It was the very best I could get, Miss Linford, and I promise you I tried in every possible way to get more."

"You have been very kind, Mr. Clarence, and I am exceedingly grateful, but as you know, three hundred twenty-two pounds will not cover my brother-in-law's debts!"

"I am aware of that, Miss Linford," Mr. Clarence replied, "but I am hoping we shall get a little more from the sale of the three paintings which I have sent to Christie's in London."

Pepita was silent, feeling that although Mr. Clarence sounded optimistic, it was very unlikely that the paintings her brother-in-law had bought because he liked the subject rather than the artist were likely to bring a large sum at an auction.

At the same time, she told herself that every little bit helped.

There were, however, the children to think of, and for the moment she felt as if she were swimming in a rough sea and it was hard to keep her head above water.

As if he realised what she was feeling, Mr. Clarence said in a gentle tone:

"I have arranged with Mr. Healey, the purchaser of the furniture, that he will not move the beds until Friday at the earliest. By that time I know you will have decided where you and the children will go."

Pepita took a deep breath.

"There is nowhere we can possibly go, Mr. Clarence, except to Scotland!"

For a moment it seemed as if she had taken Mr. Clarence's breath away.

He stared at her in astonishment before, after a perceptible pause, he said:

"Scotland? I had not thought that. . ."

"As you looked after my brother-in-law's affairs since he came here, you must be aware that when he married my sister, his father, the Duke, no only cut him off with the proverbial shilling but also expelled him from his Clan."

"Lord Alistair himself told me that," Mr. Clarence murmured.

"It was cruel and unjust, and although I myself am not Scottish, I know how much the Clan meant to my brother-in-law and how deeply he was hurt by his father's action."

Pepita's voice died away.

She was thinking how only a hard, cruel, unbending Scot could have behaved to his son as the Duke had done.

It seemed strange after all these years to look back and realise that because Lord Alistair McNairn had fallen in love with her sister, everything else that mattered to him had been taken away.

He had been punished fiercely and relentlessly for marrying for love rather than convenience.

It was a romantic story which Mr. Clarence knew without Pepita telling him what had happened.

The Duke of Strathnairn, who was sometimes spoken of as the "King of Scotland," and who certainly behaved as if he were, had a burning hatred for the English.

They had fired the fury of many Scotsmen since the battle of Culloden, and, as Lord Alistair had often said:

"Scotsmen, like elephants, never forget!"

It had been arranged for the Duke's eldest son to marry the daughter of the Chief of the McDonavan Clan, whose boundaries marched with his and with whom they had been at war for centuries.

United by their mutual hatred of the English, the Duke had agreed that Euan, the Marquis, should marry

Janet McDonavan, and the Clans would celebrate their marriage by a vast rally of the McNairns and the McDonavans, who would come from all over Scotland to attend.

But soon after the engagement was announced the Marquis was killed in a shooting accident, and, hardly waiting for the conventional short period of mourning, the Duke told his second son, Alistair, that he must take his brother's place.

"When I die you will be Chieftain of the Clan," he said, "and now you must shoulder the responsibilities of your position as your brother was ready to do and marry Janet McDonavan."

Lord Alistair was appalled at the idea.

Never for one moment had he envisaged succeeding his father as Chieftain, and he had actually spent a great deal more time in the South than his brother had.

He thought that his father's hatred of the English was out-of-date in a modern world in which there was a Queen on the throne and the traditional feuds and bitterness between the Clans had largely subsided.

However, the Duke pressed his son hard, and Alistair was torn between his own personal inclinations and his loyalty to his father.

Then quite unexpectedly he fell in love.

Looking back, even though she was very young at the time Pepita could remember seeing the two of them look at each other for the first time, and as their eyes met they had seemed to be joined by some magical spell which linked them indivisibly.

She and her sister, Denise, had been living with their father, who had retired from his position at the Foreign Office to write a book on the strange countries to which he had journeyed during his years as a Diplomat.

They had settled in a small village to the North of London in Hertfordshire.

The two girls were sitting in their garden one sunny day when there was the sound of a crash in the roadway outside, and they had sprung to their feet and run to the gate to see what had occurred.

A smart Phaeton drawn by two horses had collided with a village-cart which had come out of a side-turning without any warning because the yokel driving it was half-asleep.

It was only by a superb piece of driving, Pepita realised later, that the horses had not been badly injured, although they were plunging between the shafts, frightened by the impact.

One of the wheels from the Phaeton was lying on the road, and the vehicle itself was half-submerged in the ditch.

The village-cart being of sturdy material was not badly damaged, but the boy who had been driving it was yelling noisily.

Only as a smartly dressed, extremely handsome young man rose from the wreckage of the Phaeton was some semblance of order restored.

The horses had been brought into Sir Robert Linford's stables, and Pepita and her sister, Denise, had taken the gentleman driving them into the house, where their father had offered him a glass of wine and he had introduced himself.

"I am Alistair McNairn, and I am extremely humiliated, as you can imagine, that I should not have anticipated that country-folk expect every road on which they travel to be empty of any other traffic."

"That is true, and may I ask if you are any relation to the Duke of Strathnairn?"

"I am his son," Lord Alistair replied, "and actually I am supposed to be returning home tomorrow. This is the last time I shall be in the South for a long time."

He spoke as if he regretted it, and as his eyes were on

Denise's face, Pepita thought that whatever reasons he had had before for not wishing to leave the South, her sister had added another most compelling one.

It was not surprising that Lord Alistair should have fallen in love with Denise, for she was exceedingly beautiful, and although the two sisters resembled each other in many ways, Denise was the more spectacular.

Her hair was the gold of ripened corn, but her eyes, because their mother had French blood, were surprisingly dark.

As Lord Alistair had said afterwards to his wife:

"When once I had looked at you, my darling, I could never again see another woman's face! You are the only person I ever wanted to marry, and now that I have given you my heart, there is no possibility of retrieving it."

As he had always been known in the South as "Lord Alistair McNairn," he had not on his brother's death immediately assumed the title of Marquis.

When he refused to marry Janet McDonavan and was exiled from his home and his Clan and had, in his father's words, "dishonoured the name of his ancestors," Lord Alistair continued to be known by the title which had been his previously.

The moment he defied his father and married Denise Linford, his circumstances changed dramatically.

The Duke, who was a very rich man, had given his younger son a very generous allowance, which now immediately ceased, and all Lord Alistair was left with was a legacy he had inherited from his mother. He was, unfortunately, as turned out, allowed to draw on the capital.

Over the years this had dwindled and dwindled, and these last few months, as Pepita knew only too well, they had found it very hard to live.

She was glad now that it had not worried her brother-in-law as much as it worried her.

Because Lord Alistair was so happy with his wife and

she with him, they laughed through life, finding everything, even their poverty, amusing, and were completely confident that sooner or later "something would turn up."

Sometimes a horse they had backed in the local races would come in first, or they would manage to sell something for more money than they had paid for it.

They laughed when they visited the Pawnbrokers with the last piece of jewellery Denise had been left by her mother.

Sir Robert had never been a rich man, and while he had divided everything he possessed equally between his two daughters, they found it amounted to very little, and when Denise had spent her share she borrowed somewhat shame-facedly from Pepita's.

Pepita, however, gave her willingly what she needed.

It seemed to her only fair because after her father's death she had lived with Denise and her brother-in-law and was prepared to "pay for her keep" by helping to look after the children.

This gave Denise the chance to spend more time with her husband, and she accepted her sister's assistance gratefully.

There was a large gap between their ages, Denise being seven years older than Pepita, who was only just nineteen.

She had come to live with them in Cornwall just after her seventeenth birthday, and in the isolated village where they lived there were no eligible men to court her.

However, Pepita was happy to spend her days riding her brother-in-law's half-trained horses and playing with the children in the fields or, when they could make the effort, on the beach.

Sometimes Denise would worry about her and say:

"We cannot expect another accident on our doorstep which will provide you with a handsome stranger like Alistair! So how, dearest, will you ever find a husband?"

"I am perfectly happy as I am," Pepita would answer, "and there is no hurry."

Then Denise and Alistair had both been drowned in a storm which had swept the boat they were sailing against the treacherous rocks, and Pepita found herself frighteningly alone.

She had never thought it would be up to her to make decisions and to plan the future not only for herself but also for her sister's children.

When at first she realised she had lost Denise and her adorable brother-in-law, she could only cry despairingly and helplessly, feeling as if her whole world had come to an end.

Then because the children needed her she had forced herself to think sensibly.

It took her twenty-four hours of hard thinking to realise there was no alternative but, as she had said to Mr. Clarence, that they should go to Scotland.

Now, acutely aware of the surprise in his eyes, she went on:

"I have always understood that the Duke of Strathnairn is a rich man. I cannot believe, however cruelly he behaved towards his son, that he would allow his grandchildren to starve. As you know, Mr. Clarence, that is what will happen, unless I find somewhere for them to live."

"I thought, perhaps, Miss Linford, you would have some relations on your side of the family."

"I wish we had, but my father during the years he was a Diplomat was always living abroad, and his friends are therefore nearly all in foreign countries, including America."

Mr. Clarence laughed.

"That is certainly too far for you to go!"

"That is what I thought, and the journey to France, Italy, or Spain would be almost as expensive. No-one knows better than you do that we cannot reach even Scotland without your help."

"I of course understand that you must have some money with which to travel wherever you mean to go," Mr. Clarence said slowly, "and I have therefore set aside, Miss Linford, fifty pounds for that purpose."

"Will we really need as much as that?"

"I think it would be wise for you to have a little in hand," Mr. Clarence said tentatively.

Pepita knew he was thinking that if the Duke of Strathnairn refused to accept them, she would have to pay for their return journey to the South.

Wherever they might go, there was no assured home waiting for them, and she told herself fiercely that she would make the Duke understand that the children, if not herself, were his responsibility.

Looking at her now, Mr. Clarence thought she was far too lovely and too fragile in appearance to have such a heavy responsibility thrust upon her at her age.

At the same time, because he had known Pepita ever since she came to Cornwall, he knew she had beneath her feminine and gentle appearance a strong character.

It was stronger than that of her sister, who had relied entirely and completely upon her husband in everything she did and in every breath she drew.

Pepita, on the other hand, could be determined, and this came, Mr. Clarence thought, from the intelligence that she had inherited from her father.

He had met Sir Robert only once or twice, but he had admired him tremendously.

Although his autobiography had not sold a great number of copies, it had been praised by the Literary Critics, and Mr. Clarence, who had bought a copy, had found it immensely interesting.

"If only your father were alive," he said now.

Pepita gave him a smile that seemed to illuminate her face like the sun.

"He was so wonderful in emergencies," she said. "He always knew what to do and what to say. I suppose it was his diplomatic training, but because he was so charming, everybody always agreed to everything he suggested."

Mr. Clarence laughed.

"I think that is a gift you have inherited yourself, Miss Linford."

"I wish that were true," Pepita said. "I admit to you, Mr. Clarence, I am very, very frightened at 'bearding the lion in his den' and pointing out to the Duke of Strathnairn where his duty lies."

"I am sure you will do it with the same irresistible charm which I admired in your father," Mr. Clarence said. "And the children have inherited the same magnetic quality Lord Alistair had."

"I hope you are right," Pepita answered. "I was thinking that we should leave the day after tomorrow, which is Wednesday. I have no wish to impose further than necessary on the kindness of the gentleman who has bought the furniture."

"He is quite willing for you to stay until Friday," Mr. Clarence said.

Pepita shook her head.

"Wednesday, Thursday, or Friday. . .what does it matter?" she asked. "The unknown future is like the sword of Damocles over my head, and the sooner we set out for the North, the better!"

"If that is your decision, Miss Linford," Mr. Clarence said, "you must allow me to see to the railway-tickets and to arrange a carriage to take you and the children to Falmouth, where you will have to start the first part of your journey."

He put the papers he was holding back in his brief-case and added:

"You do not need me to tell you that it would be wise for you to take plenty of food with you, and of course rugs, as it is going to be chilly at night."

"I had thought of that," Pepita replied.

She tried to speak firmly, but there was a little quiver in her voice as she thought of how far it was to Scotland.

She was sure there would be many changes from one train to another and it would undoubtedly take a very long time.

She had only once travelled by train, when she had come from London to Cornwall, and had thought it a great adventure.

However, she was aware that travelling with two children would be very different from travelling by herself.

Rory, the eldest, was nine, and Jeanie was six, and although they were on the whole very good, she knew they would find it irksome and frustrating to be cooped up in a railway-coach or a closed carriage.

The reason Lord Alistair had settled in Cornwall was not only that living there was cheap, but also that he had been able to rent from a friend a house and several acres of land for a very small sum.

But also, Pepita suspected, he had been pleased that it was as far as possible from his father and the Clan to whom he was now the "Black Sheep."

He certainly had wanted to shake the dust of his native land off his feet and forget everything but the new life he was starting with the wife he loved to distraction.

And yet sometimes, Pepita thought, there would be a far-away look in his eyes, especially at this time of the year.

Because she was very perceptive and what the Scots would undoubtedly call "fey," she would know he was seeing the moors purple with heather, hearing the cluck of the grouse as they flighted down into the glens, or feeling the pull of the salmon on his line as he waded in the river.

She was sure too that he was thinking of the great Castle he had often described to her with its towers and turrets silhouetted against the sky, and his father's land covering thousands of acres over which the Duke reigned supreme.

Lord Alistair had said that from the Castle he was able to look out over the sea from which long ago in the past had come the raiding Vikings.

When they returned home they had left behind their fair hair and blue eyes amongst what were then the small, dark-haired men of Scotland.

Pepita often thought that her brother-in-law looked like a Viking, and the children resembled their father and their mother both, having fair hair and blue eyes. This, with her pink-and-white skin, made Jeanie look like a small angel.

Pepita often thought that it would be impossible to see two more attractive children, and she could not believe that the Duke, however hard-hearted he might be, would be able to resist them.

Anyway, Scotland was where they belonged, and to Scotland she was determined to take them.

When Mr. Clarence left, she went upstairs to their bedrooms to look rather helplessly at the enormous amount of things that still had to be packed.

She would have been extremely impractical if she left behind any of her sister's clothes when she had no money with which to buy any more for herself, and she was certain that the children would need everything they possessed.

Admittedly, many of their clothes had become too small for them, but she thought that as she was skilful with her needle she would be able to let them out and take them down at the hems.

It was frightening to think that all that stood between them and starvation was fifty pounds.

It seemed ridiculous when she looked back that her brother-in-law, Lord Alistair, had not faced the unpalatable truth that sooner or later they would have to do something about their financial situation.

She had not expected that he would owe so much money. In fact, as he had never mentioned that he had any outstanding debts, she really had not thought about it.

And why should she?

She had been brought up by her father, and by her mother when she was alive, to believe that women should always rely on a man.

He should be not only the provider of everything that was required but the organiser of their lives, planning it out the way he thought best.

This had obviously proved disastrous were her charming, happy-go-lucky brother-in-law was concerned.

When she thought of how important it was to make the Duke understand that he had to take care of them because they had literally nowhere else to go, she felt her heart beating uncomfortably.

The apprehension she had known from the moment her brother-in-law had been drowned seemed to grow until it encircled her like a dark cloud.

Nevertheless, when Wednesday morning came, the children's trunks were packed and so were her own.

"I do not want to go away!" Rory said crossly, as the man whom Mr. Clarence had sent to drive them to the station carried the trunks downstairs.

"You are going to Scotland, dearest, to see your grandfather," Pepita said. "As he lives in a big Castle, you will find it very exciting!"

"I want to stay here!" Rory answered obstinately. "This is my home and where I want to be."

As if the yearning in his voice communicated itself to Jeanie, she began to cry.

"I want my Ma-Ma!" she wailed. "Why has she gone away and left me all alone?"

Pepita knelt down and put her arms round the little girl.

"You are not alone, darling," she said, "you are with me. You have to be brave, and we are going on a big adventure, just like in a fairy-story."

Jeanie, however, was tearful, which made Pepita want to cry too.

Four hours later, when they reached the station at Falmouth, both children were intrigued by the engines puffing black smoke and by the hustle and bustle of all the passengers like themselves.

Mr. Clarence was there to see them off, and it was only when they were shown into a carriage which was comfortably upholstered that Pepita was aware that he had taken them First Class tickets.

"We cannot afford this!" she said to him, and he answered:

"The cost of your journey is a present from me and my partners, Miss Linford. We talked together, and we felt that we could not allow you and Lord Alistair's children to arrive in Scotland completely penniless. We have therefore paid your fare from here to Edinburgh. It is a tribute to the man we admired so much."

"Thank you kindly," Pepita said. "You have been so very generous, and perhaps one day I will be able to repay you in some way."

Because she felt overcome, she found it hard to express her thanks.

Then to his surprise she kissed him on the cheek.

"I shall never forget your kindness," she said.

"Take care of yourself as well as the children," he replied.

Pepita felt the tears come into her eyes and it was impossible to reply.

They climbed into the carriage, the Guard blew his whistle and waved his red flag, and Mr. Clarence took off his hat as the train moved away.

"Good-bye, Mr. Clarence!" they all cried.

Because of what he had done for them, Pepita felt a warm feeling within her breast.

Some of the apprehension that had seemed like a heavy stone growing and enlarging within her ever since her sister and brother-in-law had been drowned lightened a little.

After all, as she had said to the children, this was an adventure, and they had started out on it with an unexpected act of kindness which perhaps was a lucky augury for the future.

Because they had the carriage to themselves, the children bounced on the seats and ran from side to side as the train moved faster and faster, until Pepita thought in a way it was quite frightening.

At the same time, it was undoubtedly very much quicker than travelling in the old-fashioned manner to Scotland by road or even by sea.

Although the Cornish folk anticipated that there could be terrible accidents on the railways, she had not heard of one so far, and she only hoped that their train would not be the first.

By the time they reached London, the children, after a night and much of a day in the train, were very tired.

Although Pepita had persuaded them to lie down and try to sleep, the carriage began to fill up as they moved towards London.

The first passengers to join them were an elderly couple who obviously had no liking for children. They first eyed Rory and Jeanie with suspicion, then whispered remarks about them behind their hands.

Pepita kept the children quiet for quite a while by telling them stories, but they were not used to being constricted for hours at a time and played games with each other, Rory pretending to be a horse with Jeanie riding on his back.

At another station, an elderly gentleman joined them and his valet wrapped a rug over his knees and placed a shawl round his shoulders.

Because Rory was leaning out the window on his side of the carriage and relating excitedly what he could see on the platform, the valet said to Pepita:

"I hope, Ma'am, your children'll not make too much noise. My Master's been very ill and has to be kept as quiet as possible."

"I will do my best," Pepita answered, "but children are children, and we have already been travelling for a long time."

The valet sniffed as if that was her business.

The lady who had already shown her disapproval now said in a loud voice:

"If these trains were properly organised as they should be, there would be carriages marked for 'Children Only,' where they could be a nuisance only to themselves!"

They did not arrive in London until very late that day, the train having been delayed for over two hours.

Pepita, who was aware that they had to change stations, was terrified that the train for Scotland would leave without them.

They actually caught it with only a quarter-of-an-hour to spare.

Although it saved her from having to sit for a long time as she had expected in a gloomy Waiting-Room, she was too agitated at first to think of anything but what a rush it had been.

Once again they were lucky to start off with an empty carriage, and now as the children were tired and were unable to keep their eyes open, they fell asleep immediately.

Pepita, too, tried to stretch out on the opposite side

17

of the carriage, but although she was tired she found it hard to sleep.

When at last she had dozed off for a short time, she was awakened when they ran noisily into a station.

The engine-driver applied the brakes with an amount of jerking and crashing that made her fear that they were actually having a collision.

After that, Pepita felt as if she were moving on and on into the indefinable future, leaving behind forever the past and being at the moment in a "No-Man's Land" where it was impossible to think.

She bought food for the children when they stopped at a station since they had by now finished what they had brought in their picnic-baskets. She told them stories and tried to keep them quiet when they were joined by other passengers.

She looked out the window whenever she had the chance and made an effort to appreciate the fact that she was travelling more or less from one end of the British Isles to the other.

But by this time she felt she was nothing but a puppet being pulled on strings and had lost her individuality with the insistent noise of the turning wheels.

Life became just one long rumble, and when they finally reached Edinburgh she could hardly believe the worst part of their journey was at an end.

However, she had learnt from Mr. Clarence that there was still a long way to go before they reached Strathnairn Castle.

In fact, that part of the journey could only be undertaken by a carriage and horses.

This, Pepita was aware, was where they would need the money which Mr. Clarence had given them.

When they left the train, she went, as he had suggested, to the Station Hotel, where the children were able to wash and have a substantial breakfast seated at a table.

She asked a porter where she would be able to hire a carriage and horses to take her to Strathnairn Castle.

"It's a lang way, Ma'am," the porter replied. "It'll mean ye'll have tae stay two nights on the way, and change horses several times."

He looked at her before he finished:

"It'll cost ye an awful lot o' money."

"I realise that," Pepita said quietly.

It took the porter a long time to arrange not only the carriage and two horses to take them to the Castle, but also to haggle over what he considered would be a reasonable price with the driver.

Pepita could not help being amused and rather touched by the way he argued with the carriage owner.

When finally he told her what he had arranged, she could only be extremely grateful that he had been on her side, for it seemed, even so, to be a very large sum.

After she had given him a generous gratuity for his trouble, they set off in what she was told was a Scot's mist, which obliterated a great many of the sights she had hoped to see in the City.

As soon as they were out in the open country and the houses were left behind, Pepita had her first glimpse of Scotland and found it different from what she had expected.

She had thought she would see mountains, great fir woods, and cascading burns. It was quite a surprise to find that these came later, and the country round Edinburgh was very like England.

They spent the first night at a small, austere roadside Inn where the beds were hard but the food was plentiful and appetising, and to her relief everything was spotlessly clean.

When they set off again the next day, the children were tired, petulant, and bored with travelling.

The moment they saw their first glimpse of the moors they wanted to run and play amongst the heather and look for fish in the small twisting burns.

"There will be plenty of time to do that when we arrive," Pepita told them.

"I want to do it now!" Rory said, "I am tired of sitting in a carriage. It makes my legs ache."

Pepita thought she could say the same.

Then, after she had suggested that they should sit sideways on the seat with their legs stretched out, she found it easy to keep them amused by letting down one of the windows and getting Rory to lean out on one side and Jeanie on the other and shout to each other what they could see.

Their patience was rewarded when Rory saw a stag, and Jeanie, not to be outdone, saw what she was sure was a very large eagle.

This kept them amused for a time, and it was a relief when they stopped for meals so that they really could run about to find a small burn or search for white heather.

At the second Inn, again the food was plain but appetising, and certainly, Pepita thought, a night's rest made them all feel better-tempered.

Then they were off again. She noticed that each time the horses were changed, they seemed inferior in quality and went slower than the ones before.

Finally, when she was wondering whether she should ask the coach-driver where they could stop for tea, she had her first glimpse of the sea.

Later, looking down from the top of a sharp incline up which the horses had moved very slowly, the coach-driver gave a shout and pointed below them.

It was then that Pepita saw the Castle for the first time.

Facing the sea, the evening sun glittering on its spires and towers, which her brother-in-law had described so vividly, it had a fairy-like quality and looked, Pepita thought, much more ethereal and less formidable than she had expected.

In fact, with the purple moors behind it and the blue sea at its feet, it seemed like something out of her dreams that had no substance in reality.

"There is the Castle!" she said to the children. "That is where we are going!"

There was a note of excitement in her voice which made their eyes follow the direction in which she was pointing her finger.

"Is that Grandpapa's Castle?" Jeanie asked.

"That was where your Da-Da lived when he was a boy like Rory," Pepita replied.

The children looked at it solemnly as the horses began the descent down the other side of the hill up which they had climbed so laboriously.

"How long are we going to stay at the Castle, Aunt Pepita?" Rory asked.

As it was a question she had asked herself, Pepita had no idea of the answer, and she knew that the only person who could reply to the question would be the Duke.

Then, because she was more frightened than she would even dare to admit to herself, she began to pray:

"Please, God, let us stay. Please, God, please. . ."

Chapter Two

As the horses trotted on towards the Castle, Pepita became more and more frightened.

She had realised at their last stop that she had very little money left except the generous sum she had already put aside in an envelope to give to the coach-driver for the whole journey.

What she had not expected was that she would have to pay for the new horses at each posting-place.

Also, by the time she had paid the bills for the night and the food they ate wherever there was an available Inn, the fifty pounds which Mr. Clarence had given her had dwindled to a mere pittance.

She told herself it was what she might have expected since she was very bad at handling money, having always left everything to do with it first to her father, then to her brother-in-law.

Now when her journey was almost at an end she began to think that it had been a mistake to arrive without having first notified the Duke.

She had not done so because she had been afraid it would have given him the chance of refusing to accept his grandchildren, which she had known would be much more difficult for him to do once they had actually arrived in Scotland.

At the same time, she was aware that she was more frightened than she had ever been before in her whole life.

She thought frantically that if only she herself had some money, she could take the children somewhere where she could look after them and care for them, and Lord Alistair's unkind relatives need not be involved.

Then her intelligence told her that this would be impossible since Rory would have to go to School, and if he was to be educated in the same way that his father had been, it would not only cost money but would require the influence of somebody distinguished to ensure that he was accepted as a suitable pupil.

Once again she felt herself crying out at the injustice that Lord Alistair had been exiled because he had fallen in love and that both he and her sister had suffered because as far as the Duke was concerned they did not exist.

But the children, tired, petulant, and hungry, were very real.

She tidied Jeanie's hair and thought that with her little poke-bonnet she looked very sweet and attractive.

Rory had also become rather ruffled, and she did her best to smarten him up, even though, like all boys, he resented her fussing over him.

As she finished she was aware that the horses were turning through some impressive wrought-iron gates with lodges on each side which looked like small Castles, and moving down a long avenue with fir-trees on either side of it.

At the end she could see the Castle, and because it was so large and so very impressive it made her gasp.

It was, she thought, exactly the sort of Castle she had imagined would belong to the Duke of Strathnairn.

She could see his standard flying from the highest tower and knew that on the other side of it there was the North Sea stretching out blue but turbulent towards what had once been the land of the Vikings.

The coachman brought the horses to a standstill under a large portico beneath which was a huge oak door studded with brass nails.

As the horses stopped the door opened, and Pepita saw standing on the steps a kilted figure looking at them with an expression of surprise.

"The Castle is very big!" Rory remarked in a slightly awe-struck voice.

It was what Pepita was feeling herself, and as the carriage-door was opened and she stepped out, she hoped she did not appear as terrified as she felt.

The kilted figure, who she guessed must be the Butler, bowed.

"Good-evening, Ma'am?" he said, and it was more of a question than a greeting.

"I wish to see the Duke of Strathnairn."

She thought there was a slight tremor in her voice, but she held her chin high and hoped she had an air of authority about her.

"I do na think His Grace is expecting ye, Ma'am."

The Butler had a broad Scottish accent, and Pepita was aware that the children were staring at him with obvious curiosity.

"Will you inform His Grace that I have brought his grandchildren to him?"

If Pepita had meant to startle the Butler, she certainly succeeded.

For a moment he stared at her as if he thought he had not understood what she was saying. Then he asked:

24

"Are ye saying, Ma'am, that these are Lord Alistair's bairns?"

"Yes, that is right."

As she spoke, Pepita saw the Butler's expression change.

He looked first at Rory, then at Jeanie, in a manner which told her he was delighted by them.

Because she knew she had found an ally, Pepita said, putting a hand on the small boy's shoulder:

"This is Rory, and this is Jeanie."

As if this broke the spell that had kept Jeanie silent, she said:

"I's tired an' I's thirsty!"

"We'll do something aboot that in a moment," the Butler said, "an' if ye're tired, I'd best carry ye up the stairs."

He picked Jeanie up in his arms as he spoke, and she did not protest but said:

"I's too tired to walk."

"O' course ye are," the Butler said, "an' it's a lang way to England."

He went ahead of them and Pepita saw there was a staircase of white stone leading up to the First Floor.

She remembered as they climbed it that her brother-in-law had told her that in all grand Scottish houses the important rooms were on the First Floor.

There was a large landing with a fireplace in which a huge log was burning, and the Butler put Jeanie down on her feet outside two lofty double doors.

Then he smiled at Pepita as if to reassure her before he opened one of them and walked inside.

In a voice that seemed almost unnaturally loud he announced:

"The Earl of Nairn and Lady Jean, Your Grace."

It surprised Pepita that he should use the children's titles, which she had not thought of before, because Lord

Alistair had never assumed his brother's place after he was killed.

Vaguely she remembered hearing that on the death of a Duke's eldest son, the Marquisate went into abeyance, but his children had courtesy titles.

For the moment, however, because she was so afraid, the room seemed to swim round her and she was aware of nothing but the evening sun coming through the three tall windows.

Then she saw there were three people at the far end of the room in front of a marble fireplace.

As she took Jeanie by the hand and drew her forward, she was aware that there was one man whom it was impossible not to notice and not to realise who he was.

There was some resemblance to her brother-in-law in his height, the squareness of his shoulders, and the carriage of his head.

But otherwise, the Duke, with his grey hair, lined face, and tight, thin lips, had, she thought, the tyrannical look she had expected of him.

There was absolute silence as she and the two children walked slowly to the end of the room, which seemed a very long way.

Then as they came within a few feet of the Duke he asked sharply:

"What are you doing here and why have you brought these children to me?"

His voice, Pepita thought, was as frightening as his appearance, but with a tremendous effort she managed to reply quietly but clearly:

"I brought them to Your Grace because there is nowhere else for them to go."

"What do you mean by that?" the Duke enquired.

"Their father and mother are both. . .dead."

She knew as she spoke that it was a shock to him, for

even thought his expression did not change she knew he stiffened.

For a moment there was complete silence. Then as if it frightened Jeanie she said:

"I's tired! I want to go home!"

"Then that is where you had better take her!" the Duke said to Pepita. "As far as I am concerned, I have no grandchildren!"

Pepita drew in her breath.

"That is not true, Your Grace! They are here! They exist! And although your treatment of their father made him very unhappy, I cannot believe you would want these small children to suffer."

As if what she said infuriated the Duke, his eyes darkened and he scowled at her as he said:

"Take them away! You brought them here without my permission, and you can go back where you came from!"

The way he spoke was so ferocious that for a moment Pepita felt her voice had died in her throat.

Then as if his hostility communicated itself to the children, Rory slipped his hand into Pepita's and said:

"Let us go home. They do not want us here!"

Pepita's fingers closed over his and Jeanie suddenly sat down on the floor.

"I's tired and I's thirsty," she said, "and I want my Da-Da!"

She burst into tears, and Pepita released Rory's hand and knelt down beside her.

"Do not cry, my darling," she said. "I am sure your grandfather before he turns us out onto the moors will at least give you a drink of water!"

As she spoke she picked Jeanie up in her arms and looked up at the Duke, who seemed an enormous height above her, to say:

"I should be grateful, Your Grace, if the children could have something to eat and drink before we are

thrown out of the Castle! We have been travelling for
nearly a week, having come from Cornwall."

There was something about her request that made
the Duke undecided how to answer. Then as if bored with
the conflict between them Rory said:

"Papa had a sporran just like yours!"

His fear of the Duke seemed to be forgotten and he
walked nearer to him and said:

"Papa said that sporrans were made of otter, but
yours is different."

Somehow, despite his animosity, the Duke had to
make some explanation, and he said coldly:

"Mine is a Chieftain's sporran."

"Papa said a Chieftain is the father of his Clan, and
that all the McNairns have to obey their Chieftain."

"That is right," the Duke replied.

Pepita stood still with Jeanie in her arms.

The child was very tired and now her head was
nodding, her eyes closing.

Pepita did not speak, she merely looked at the Duke,
and after a moment he said, as if every word was wrenched
from between his lips:

"I suppose you will have to stay here the night.
Torquil, take them to Mrs. Sutherland."

Because she had been so bemused by the Duke,
Pepita had not looked at the other people who were with
him and who had sat silent and immobile while the battle
between them had been taking place.

Now a young man rose from one of the armchairs and
she saw that he was tall, handsome, and was also wearing
a kilt of the McNairn tartan.

He smiled at her, then reached out his arms to take
Jeanie from her.

"I am sure the child is too heavy for you," he said. "I
will carry her."

Jeanie, who was almost asleep, did not protest.

Then as Pepita looked for Rory, she heard him say to the Duke:

"I want to see a claymore! Papa said you had lots and lots of claymores in the Castle, but we did not have one at home!"

There was a pause before the Duke replied:

"You can see one tomorrow."

He had spoken as if the words were dragged from him. At the same time, Pepita thought the scowl had gone from his face.

She took Rory by the hand and when she had done so looked up at the Duke.

"I thank Your Grace," she said and curtseyed.

She thought the expression in his eyes when he looked at her was hard.

At the same time, she was so relieved to have won at least a respite that her only thought was not to antagonise him any further at the moment, but to find food for the children and rest for them all.

The Butler was on the landing outside the door and she knew he was waiting to hear whether they were to stay or to go.

She took from her hand-bag the envelope which held the money she had promised to pay for the journey from Edinburgh, and gave it to him, saying:

"Will you please thank the coachman, and this is what I owe him."

She thought by his smile that he understood what had happened and was delighted.

"I'll hae yer luggage brought tae yer rooms, Ma'am," he said.

Torquil McNairn, who was carrying Jeanie, was already halfway down the passage, and Pepita hurried after them.

As if the news of their arrival had alerted the servants in the Castle that something unusual was happening, before they had gone very far an elderly woman came hurrying towards them.

The first sight of her black satin apron and the chatelaine hanging from her waist told Pepita that she was the Housekeeper.

"I have a guest for you, Mrs. Sutherland," Torquil McNairn said, "who is very tired and also very thirsty."

"I heard that Lord Alistair's bairns had arrived," Mrs. Sutherland replied, "but I couldna believe it tae be true."

"It is true," he answered. "Now, Mrs. Sutherland, where are you going to put them?"

Mrs. Sutherland looked at Pepita, who held out her hand.

"My name is Linford," she said, "and I am Rory and Jeanie's aunt."

Mrs. Sutherland dropped her a small curtsey.

"Guid-evening, Ma'am, and welcome tae Strathnairn Castle! It's a great surprise, a great surprise indeed, as we've no heard frae His Lordship for monny a year."

"Lord Alistair is dead," Pepita said, "and so is my sister, the children's mother!"

Mrs. Sutherland gave a cry of horror.

"I canna believe it!" she said. "We were never told!"

Then as if she felt that what had to be said could be said later, she turned and walked down a passage ahead of them, and stopping at one door opened it to say:

"I think it's right that His Young Lordship should have his father's room."

It was a large and impressive room with a carved four-poster bed, the windows looking out over the bay.

"That settles you, young man," Torquil McNairn said. "Now, Mrs. Sutherland, what about Miss Linford and this little door-mouse I am carrying?"

"I suggest they awl stay next door to each other," Mrs. Sutherland replied in a practical tone.

She opened the next door and said to Pepita:

"Ye'll be comfortable enough here, Ma'am, an' ye've a door into Her Ladyship's room."

"That will be very nice," Pepita said. "She is used to sleeping alone, but she might be frightened in a strange place."

Torquil McNairn carried Jeanie through the communicating door which Mrs. Sutherland opened for him, and he laid the child, who was by this time fast asleep, very gently down on the bed.

As he did so, Mrs. Sutherland said:

"I'll see to the luggage and get the housemaids to come and unpack what ye need immediately."

She bustled away, and Pepita found herself facing Torquil McNairn and thinking he was a very handsome and attractive man.

She guessed his age to be about twenty-seven or twenty-eight, because although he seemed young in comparison to the Duke, there was something authoritative and in a way dominating about him which would have been unlikely if he had been very young.

He smiled at her and said:

"You have certainly caused a sensation!"

As she supposed he must know how her brother-in-law had been exiled, she replied:

"I thought, and obviously correctly, that if I asked if I could bring the children here, the answer would be 'No!' "

"So you just arrived, as if from another Planet!"

"Is that how it seems to you? I certainly feel as if we crossed half the world to get here!"

"I am not surprised you are feeling tired if you have come all the way from Cornwall," he said.

Then in a different tone he added:

"I am desperately sorry to hear of Alistair's death. What happened?"

"Both he. . .and my sister were. . .drowned!"

There was an unmistakable tremor in Pepita's voice,

because it was still hard to speak of it without feeling that she wanted to cry.

"Is there nobody else to look after the children but you?"

"Nobody!" she answered. "And we could not continue to stay in their home as I would have liked to do, because there was no money."

He stared at her as if he could not believe what she had said.

Then as she thought that perhaps she had been wrong in confiding in a stranger, Pepita asked:

"Would it be rude to enquire what relation you are to Alistair?"

"I am his cousin, but I am here only as a guest. My home is about ten miles away to the North."

As he finished speaking, Rory interrupted them by running in through the door which led out into the corridor.

"You must come to look," he said to Pepita. "I can see a ship from my bedroom window!"

"Be careful not to lean out," Pepita warned him quickly. "You are not used to a house which is so high off the ground."

"Do you think it is a fishing-boat?" Rory asked. "Papa said there were lots of them here in the sea and they come back to port filled with hundreds and hundreds of fish."

Pepita looked at Torquil McNairn as if she expected him to supply the answer to Rory's question.

As if he understood, he said:

"I suggest before you worry about ships you come with me and we will find somebody to give you a drink and something to eat. You may have to wait a little time for your supper, but I am sure you are hungry."

"I am very hungry!" Rory said firmly. "I would like a bannock with lots of butter and heather honey!"

This was something they had sampled only since they

had arrived in Scotland, and Pepita gave a little laugh before she said:

"Please, we do not want to be any bother."

"It is no bother," Torquil McNairn replied. "Come along, young man. We will find you some food and make sure you no longer have that empty feeling inside you."

They went off together, and as Torquil McNairn gave her a smile before he disappeared, Pepita felt she had found at least one friend.

It was a joy she had not expected to have no less than three young housemaids unpacking her clothes and the children's.

When Mrs. Sutherland said they should leave most things for tomorrow, she felt that they had moved in and it might be difficult for the Duke to dislodge them.

Pepita undressed Jeanie and gave her a little warm milk to drink, but the child was too exhausted to need anything more.

Only when she was fast asleep and tucked up cosily in a comfortable bed could Pepita think about herself.

"Ye'll have to change for dinner in a few minutes," Mrs. Sutherland said, "and I expect ye'd like a bath after yer lang journey."

"I think first I should ask if I am to dine with His Grace," Pepita replied.

"Och, aye, Ma'am!" Mrs. Sutherland exclaimed as if she was shocked at the idea that she might not do so.

Pepita, however, was far from certain, and although she was convinced by Mrs. Sutherland that it was expected, she was apprehensive when finally she walked down the passage towards the Chieftain's room.

Before this she had said good-night to Rory, who, having eaten his supper, had put himself to bed.

She knew he could not stay up any later in spite of all the new things there were for him to see, because his head was nodding.

Finally, without making any fuss about it, he agreed to go to sleep and leave everything else to be discovered tomorrow.

Because she was so nervous of what was waiting for her, Pepita, having had her bath in front of the fire in her bedroom and enjoying feeling the tiredness soak away from her in the warm water, chose the first gown she found hanging in her wardrobe.

It was a very pretty one which had belonged to her sister but was rather more sophisticated than anything she owned herself.

She thought this was a good thing because she wished to appear capable of giving the children their lessons, as she had done while they were living in Cornwall.

At the back of her mind all the time they had travelled to Scotland was the fear that as she was a hated Sassenach, the Duke would immediately dispense with her services.

Because the idea frightened her even more than she was frightened already, she tried not to think of it.

She knew that with no money and no previous experience of earning her living it was going to be very difficult for her to do so.

Once again she felt that no-one could assist her except God, who had at least brought them to safety from Cornwall to Scotland.

She therefore prayed as she walked down the corridor that the Duke, if he accepted the children, would not transfer onto her his hatred and dislike of everything that was English.

The Duke was waiting for her in the room in which they had been talking when they arrived.

If he had looked awe-inspiring and magnificent then, in his evening-clothes with his lace jabot at his throat and the velvet coat with its silver buttons he looked very much a Chieftain.

34

As she walked towards him Pepita did not miss the glint of topaz in the top of his skean-dhu, which was thrust into the top of his tartan hose, and saw that his sporran was even more ornate and impressive than the one Rory had noticed.

Because she had been so afraid of being late, Mrs. Sutherland had helped her dress, and now she found that the Duke was alone in the room and there was no sign of Torquil McNairn or the other person who had been there when they arrived.

Because she had been so agitated and upset by the Duke's reception, she had only vaguely realised that the other person was a woman, and she wondered what relation she was to the two men.

Now as she curtseyed to the Duke she could think only of him and was aware that while he was not scowling at her as ferociously as he had before, there was nevertheless an expression of hostility in his eyes, and his mouth was set in a hard line.

"I hope, Miss Linford," he said, "that you have been well looked after."

She was quite certain there was a sarcastic note in his voice, but she replied:

"Everybody has been very kind, Your Grace, and as you must have realised, the children were desperately tired. They are very young to have attempted such a long journey."

"A journey which was quite unnecessary!" the Duke said loftily.

"On the contrary, Your Grace, there was no alternative!"

"Why not?"

The question was sharp.

"Because I could no longer pay the rent for the house in which they were living, and the furniture, the horses, and everything else my brother-in-law possessed had to be sold to meet his debts."

She hoped this would surprise the Duke, and she thought his lips tightened. She was aware that he looked at her sharply, almost as if he questioned whether she was telling the truth.

Then as if he was too curious to keep silent he said:

"Alistair had his mother's money!"

"It was all spent, Your Grace, and so was everything my sister owned, and, as it happens, everything I myself possessed."

She thought the Duke was not convinced. Then he said:

"I find it hard to understand how this was possible, unless there was some sort of wild extravagance."

"There was no extravagance," Pepita replied, "but things are not as cheap as they used to be, or perhaps as they are in Scotland. I assure you my brother-in-law did not indulge himself in any way, but we had to eat!"

She spoke almost sharply because she felt the Duke was being unnecessarily critical.

It also made her angry to think that when everything in the Castle was extremely luxurious, her sister had had to pinch and save to have even a little comfort in their home.

Alistair had never been able to afford to buy the horses he would have liked to own.

Almost as if he was aware of her thoughts, the Duke said:

"Whatever happened, it was of my son's choosing."

"That is true, Your Grace, and he never regretted it. But I know how homesick he was sometimes for Scotland, and while he was very happy with my sister, he missed his own people."

She spoke very softly, feeling it would be impossible for the Duke to take exception to what she said.

Then, before the Duke could reply, Torquil McNairn came into the room and with him was the woman Pepita

36

had not been able to notice properly when they had arrived.

She was fairly young, perhaps about thirty, Pepita thought, and one glance told her that she was carrying a child.

"Oh, there you are, my dear!" the Duke said as she approached. "I suppose now I should introduce you to our unexpected guest. This, as you know, is Miss Linford, Alistair's sister-in-law."

"I gathered that," was the reply, "and I suppose she is aware that I am your wife!"

Pepita was in fact astonished since this was certainly something she had not expected.

She had known that Alistair's mother had died when he was quite young, but she was sure he had never anticipated for one moment that his father would marry again.

Now as she looked at the Duchess she saw that she was plain and had what one might describe as a "homely" face.

She had the rather ugly red hair that was almost sandy, and as her eye-lashes were the same it gave her a somewhat ferret-like look.

Pepita curtseyed but the Duchess did not put out her hand, and as she rose she was aware that if the Duke disliked her, so did his new wife.

"Dinner is served, Your Grace!" the Butler announced from the door.

The Duchess, without saying anything to Pepita, turned to the Duke and linked her arm in his.

"I did hope," she said in a voice that seemed unnaturally loud, "that we would be able to have a quiet dinner tonight, with just ourselves, but now we are quite a party!"

There was no doubt that she was being disagreeable, and Pepita wondered if it would not have been better for her to have had something to eat in her bedroom, but it was too late now to suggest it.

Then as the Duke and Duchess moved towards the door, she realised that Torquil was waiting for her, and as she looked at him he smiled and she saw that his eyes were twinkling.

As they walked behind their host and hostess, he said in such a low voice that only she could hear, just one word:

"Jealous!"

Dinner was delicious, and as Pepita was hungry she enjoyed every mouthful of the salmon caught that day and the grouse which had been shot on the Duke's moors.

Only after the Piper had gone round the table playing the bagpipes and accepted the traditional dram of whisky from the Duke in a silver cup was she aware that she and the Duchess would leave the room together.

She had said very little during dinner, mostly because the Duke talked as if it was his right and he had no wish to listen to anybody else.

Also, because she was sitting opposite her hostess on the left of the Duke, Pepita was acutely aware that every time the Duchess looked at her, the animosity in her eyes increased.

Torquil, on the other hand, was amusing and witty and actually made the Duke laugh several times, although it was obviously somewhat of an effort.

By the time the meal had finished, Pepita could not help thinking that the atmosphere, of which she was very conscious, was her fault, and that both the right and the dignified thing to do would be for her to leave the Castle as soon as it was possible to do so.

Then she knew that to leave the children would be wrong and something which both her sister and brother-in-law would beg her not to do.

'Perhaps if they treated me as an ordinary Governess,' she thought, 'I could stay in the School-Room.'

Then she remembered that the Duke might turn them all out tomorrow, and even if their visit was extended, they were obviously very unwelcome, and she would never have a happy moment after she had left if he decided to exile Rory and Jeanie as he had his own son.

'I must save them,' she thought frantically. 'Somehow I must save them.'

When she and the Duchess had reached the Drawing-Room and the latter had lowered herself carefully into an armchair in front of the fire, she said sharply:

"I hope, Miss Linford, that although my husband has offered you his hospitality for the night, you are making plans to leave as soon as possible."

"I had hoped, Your Grace," Pepita said very quietly, "that the children would be allowed to make this their home as there is nowhere else available."

"That is impossible," the Duchess said, "quite, quite impossible!"

Then, as if she thought Pepita did not understand, she added:

"This will be the home of *my* children, and I have no wish to be disturbed by usurpers or cuckoos in the nest!"

As she spoke, Pepita understood, and she felt she had been very stupid not to realise before what was upsetting the Duchess.

If she gave birth to a son he still would not be the heir to the Dukedom or Chieftain of the Clan, because the succession would go to the offspring of the Duke's eldest son.

Pepita could understand the Duchess's resentment at their unexpected appearance, but there was nothing she could do about it.

But whatever the Duke and Duchess might feel, Rory was now in a very important position.

Pepita knew, with a sudden determination she had never had before, that she would fight for his rights and would not allow him to be sent away ignominiously or ignored as his father had been.

She therefore did not reply to the Duchess but realised how irritated she was by the way she was tapping her fingers on the arm of her chair and staring into the fire as if the flames echoed the anger which was obviously seething within her.

Because she was worried, although it seemed impossible that the Duchess might be unkind to the children, Papita said:

"I am sorry if our coming here has upset Your Grace, but honestly there was nothing else I could do. I felt that however incensed the Duke might have been with his son, he would not wish his grandchildren to starve through no fault of their own."

"Very plausible, Miss Linford!" the Duchess said sneeringly. "But you cannot be so thick-skinned as not to realise that there is no room for grandchildren in the Castle, and certainly no room for a Sassenach!"

Before Pepita could think of how she could reply, to her relief the door opened and they were joined by the Duke and Torquil McNairn.

Because she felt she could not bear any more or face up to yet another cross-examination, she rose to her feet.

"I hope, Your Grace," she said to the Duke, "that you will forgive me if I retire. Like the children I am very tired, and I feel as if the wheels are still rolling under me."

She tried to speak lightly, but instead her voice sounded weak and rather helpless.

"Of course go to bed, Miss Linford," the Duke said. "And tomorrow we must discuss what can be done about this situation."

"Thank you," Pepita said. "Thank you too, very much,

for having us. I was very, very frightened that we might have to sleep on the beach or in the heather!"

Because she was speaking with a sincerity which she could not help, she thought for a moment that the Duke was at a loss for words.

Then she curtseyed to him and to the Duchess, who ignored her, and turned towards the door.

Torquil McNairn was there before her and opened it.

Then as she gave him a little smile of thanks he said very quietly:

"You are wonderful! Go to sleep and do not worry!"

She felt that his words touched her heart, and some of the apprehension which had enveloped her since the Duchess's unpleasantness melted away.

Then as she ran down the passage to her own room, she could think of nothing except that for the moment she had achieved her objective.

She and the children had reached Scotland, and at least, even if it was only for the night, they were safe.

Chapter Three

$\mathcal{M}$rs. Sutherland called Pepita at seven-thirty in the morning, telling her that breakfast was at eight-thirty and the Duke expected everybody to be in the Breakfast-Room on time.

Pepita, who was still feeling sleepy even though she had had a good night, jumped up quickly.

"I expect the children are still asleep," she said, "and I will not wake them for another half-an-hour."

"It must ha' been a terrible journey for ye awl," Mrs. Sutherland said sympathetically.

"It was rather exhausting," Pepita answered, "and I was worried about what would happen when we arrived."

"It was a real shock for us, Miss," Mrs. Sutherland said confidentially. "We'd heard His Lordship were wed, but we hadna heard he had two bonny wee bairns, and I'm sure His Grace will learn tae be proud o' them."

"I hope so," Pepita said doubtfully.

She wondered if she should tell Mrs. Sutherland how

frightened she was that the Duke might decide to send them away, then she thought that would be indiscreet.

She could only pray that what Mr. Clarence had called "their father's magnetic charm" would somehow make all three of them more welcome than they had been yesterday.

After she had dressed Jeanie, and with Rory wildly excited about what he could see from his bedroom window, she took the children along the corridor to the Breakfast-Room, which was on the same floor as the Drawing-Room and Dining-Room, but looked out over the moors.

She was relieved to find when she entered that only the Duke and Torquil McNairn were there and there was no sign of the Duchess.

Thinking over what had happened last night, she had come to the conclusion that her more dangerous enemy was the Duchess.

She could understand that for her it must have been more of a shock even than for the Duke to learn that Lord Alistair had a son.

Torquil McNairn rose as she came into the room, but the Duke remained seated.

Because Pepita had told them what to do, the children went up to his side. Rory bowed and Jeanie curtseyed as they said:

"Good-morning, Grandpapa!"

She thought the Duke was surprised at their good manners, but he replied with a gruff "Good-morning!" then looked at her from under his eye-brows.

She also curtseyed as she said:

"Good-morning, Your Grace. I am sorry if we are a little late."

"As it happens it is we who are early," Torquil McNairn said, "because the Duke and I are going fishing."

Rory gave a cry that was almost a shout and said:

"I can fish! I want to catch a salmon!"

Then before anybody could speak he added:

"Please, Grandpapa, I want to learn to shoot. Papa said he would teach me when I was nine, and I had my birthday three weeks ago!"

"You are too young," the Duke said sharply.

"Papa shot when he was nine, and you taught him how. He told me so!" Rory answered sturdily.

There was silence. Then Torquil laughed.

"There is nothing you can say to that. Actually, my father allowed me to carry a gun for the first time on my ninth birthday."

"Then I can shoot?" Rory asked. "Please say I can shoot!"

Pepita thought as she sat down at the breakfast-table that it would be difficult for anybody to resist the pleading in Rory's voice.

Moreover, as he stood beside his grandfather she saw that there was a very obvious likeness between them.

"I will think about it," the Duke conceded finally.

Somewhat reluctantly, as if he wished to go on arguing about it, Rory sat down at the table, and the Butler, who Pepita had learnt from Mrs. Sutherland was called Fergus, put a bowl of porridge in front of him.

"I do not suppose you know what that is," the Duke said.

"It is porridge," Rory answered, "and Papa said all good Scotsmen eat porridge and should be standing while they do so."

Pepita smiled.

She remembered her brother-in-law telling the children that Scotsmen ate their porridge standing in case they were suddenly attacked by another Clan, when if they were sitting down they might be caught at a disadvantage.

She was aware, because he did not say anything, that the Duke was surprised at Rory's answer, and she said to him in a quiet voice:

"As I think it is unlikely anybody will attack you at this moment, it would be easier and far cleaner to eat sitting down."

"But it is not the right way to eat porridge in Scotland," Rory said seriously.

"I know that," Pepita replied, "but your grandfather, who is the Chieftain, is eating his at the table, and I think we shall all be safe."

As if he was pacified by what she had said, Rory started to eat from the bowl in front of him, but Jeanie pushed hers to one side.

"I do not like porridge."

"If you say that, you are a Sassenach!" Rory said. "Grandpapa hates Sassenachs!"

Pepita looked quickly at the Duke, feeling that he might be angry, but she saw there was a faint smile quivering at the corners of his mouth.

Although she did not say anything, Fergus took the porridge away from Jeanie and gave her instead a salmon fishcake.

She ate that with relish, and Pepita thought she had never known the children to eat a larger breakfast.

When they had only half-finished, Torquil said:

"The gillies will be waiting. I think I had better go ahead if I am to begin at the top of the river."

"I will start at the bottom," the Duke said, "but I want to speak to Miss Linford before I leave."

Pepita's heart gave a little jerk, but as he walked towards the door Torquil smiled at her as if to tell her, as he had last night, not to worry.

However, she was not so much worried as frightened, and when the children had finished their breakfast she told Rory he could go to explore the garden.

"I want to go fishing with Grandpapa!" he answered stubbornly. "Ask him if I can go with him, Aunt Pepita, and tell him I can fish very well."

He had in fact been taught by his father to fish for trout in the small stream that ran through the Estate in Cornwall.

The trout had of course been quite small, but at least Rory knew how to handle a rod and to reel in his line once a fish was on the hook.

"I will try," Pepita said to the small boy, "but do not be disappointed if your grandfather refuses."

Fergus heard the last part of the conversation, and he said now:

"Ye stay wi' me, M'Lord, an' I'll show you His Grace's skean-dhus."

"I would like that," Rory said, "and I want to see a claymore."

Fergus laughed.

"There are plenty in the Chieftain's room."

"Then please take me there, and can I hold one in my hand?"

Fergus promised him he could, and as they walked away Pepita took Jeanie back to their bedroom, where she hoped she would find Mrs. Sutherland.

She was, however, told by the housemaid that she was in the Housekeeper's room, which was at the end of the corridor.

It was a bright room, filled, Pepita saw at a glance, with souvenirs that Mrs. Sutherland must have collected all her life.

There were sketches hung on the walls that looked as if they had been drawn by children, bunches of white heather, some of which was brown with age, as well as small Highland bonnets that she suspected had been worn by Alistair and his brother when they were Rory's age.

There were also black cock feathers and white ones from ptarmigan.

She knew Jeanie would be fascinated by such an array

of strange objects and Mrs. Sutherland would have no difficulty in looking after her.

Pepita therefore walked quickly back along the corridor, feeling as if she were a School-girl about to be reprimanded.

The Duke was waiting for her not in the Drawing-Room but in the room next to it, which she learnt was his special sanctum and known quite simply as "The Duke's Room."

Books covered one wall and on the others between the windows were paintings of previous Dukes, all of whom looked, she thought, not only autocratic but fierce and war-like.

At the same time, although she was afraid of him, she could not help admiring the Duke as he stood with his back to the fireplace.

He looked very impressive in his kilt, worn in the daytime with a tweed jacket, and his sporran was what Rory had expected to see, plain with the head of an otter on it.

The Duke did not speak as she walked down the room towards him, and when she reached him there was a perceptible pause, as if he intended to make her feel uncomfortable.

"Sit down, Miss Linford," he said at last.

Thankfully, not only because her legs felt weak but because he was so tall that she had to look up at him, Pepita sat down on the sofa.

Again there was a pause before he said slowly:

"I would like to start by saying that I consider it an extraordinary and reprehensible action on your part to have arrived here without first notifying me of your intention to do so!"

"I brought the children to you," Pepita replied, "because it was impossible for them to stay any longer in Cornwall and there was nowhere we could go or where they belonged."

"You must be aware that after he left I considered that Alistair was no longer my son," the Duke said harshly.

"That was your personal decision," Pepita answered, "but legally, morally, and because his blood was your blood, he still belonged to you."

She spoke quietly, without anything aggressive in her tone, but the Duke glared at her as if he thought she was being impertinent.

Then she asked:

"What was I to do with two small children who had been left without a penny to their name?"

"You said that last night," the Duke replied, "but I can hardly believe it is true."

"I swear to you, if you like on the Bible, that all we possess at this moment is exactly three sovereigns and five shillings!" Pepita answered. "What is more, my brother-in-law's Solicitors will tell you, if you communicate with them, that there are still debts outstanding of over two hundred pounds, which will have to be paid sometime."

"I will not be responsible for my son's debts! They were incurred because he married an Englishwoman!" the Duke exclaimed.

Pepita looked round the comfortable room, which she saw was furnished with every luxury.

She thought that the sale of the flat-topped Georgian desk or just one of the paintings on the wall, all painted by great artists, would not only cover what her brother-in-law owed but would also leave a great deal over.

Then because the way the Duke was behaving made her feel angry, and especially because she thought that his sneering at her sister was unforgivable, she said in a voice which she attempted to keep quiet and controlled:

"I have a solution to this problem, Your Grace, if you will listen to it."

"What is it?" he asked.

"If you will give me some money, not very much, but

enough to rent a house for the children where I can look after them, I will endeavour to bring them up in the way your son would have wanted me to."

She paused for a moment, and when the Duke did not speak she went on:

"The only matter in which I would need your help is to get Rory into a good Public School and if possible to University. He is very intelligent, and if he is to earn his own living, as appears likely, he will certainly need a good education."

As she finished speaking, the Duke stared at her as if she were some strange phenomenon he had never seen before.

Then he asked harshly:

"Do you really think that is something a young woman of your age could do? And what will happen to the children if you marry?"

"I am not concerned with myself," Pepita said, "but with two small children who so far in their lives have known only love and will not be able to cope with being disliked or punished for something their father did before they were born."

The Duke, who had been standing in front of the fire, sat down in the seat opposite Pepita, and after staring at her for some seconds from under his eye-brows he said:

"You surprise me, Miss Linford!"

"Why?"

"Because, although I can hardly believe what you are saying, you are prepared to take on what I should have thought would have seemed too formidable a task for any woman of your age with no man to look after her and protect her."

"I admit it will be frightening, Your Grace, but I am certain I can do it. Moreover, in many ways it would be better for the children than to stay here, where they are not wanted."

He did not answer her, then suddenly and sharply he said:

"Why was I not told that Alistair had a son?"

His voice seemed to echo round the Study. As Pepita stared at him, thinking it was a stupid question, suddenly with a perception she had always had she knew what had occurred.

Because the Duke had lost his eldest son, the Marquis, and had excluded Alistair from his life, he had been desperate to have another son. Even if he could not take his title, he could be Chieftain of the Clan.

He had therefore married a woman much younger than himself, and Pepita guessed that the Duchess was a member of the same Clan he had tried to force on his sons in the hope that she would provide him with an heir.

Suddenly Pepita could understand as she had not been able to do before how much the arrival of Rory had confused the Duke's plans.

He was waiting now for an answer to his question, and after a moment Pepita said quietly:

"When my brother-in-law learnt that his elder brother was dead, since you had cut him out of the family he did not assume his title. Although I know he was desperately sorry he had lost his brother and you your son, he thought you would think it a presumption if he communicated with you."

She paused. Then she added:

"Surely it would have been your place to find him? You knew that when you died he would succeed to the Dukedom, and it seems extraordinary that just because you hated my sister you did nothing to demolish the barrier you had erected between them and you."

She thought as she finished speaking that the Duke would roar at her for telling him what was the truth.

Instead he said obstinately, almost as if he was speaking to himself:

"I will never forgive Alistair for disobeying not only his father but his Chieftain!"

Pepita gave a little laugh, and as the Duke stared at her she said:

"Your Grace may have an omnipotent power over your Clan, but there is something in life which is even higher than a man's loyalty to his father, to whom he has sworn allegiance."

The Duke did not ask the question, but she knew he was waiting to hear it.

"It is something called 'Love,' Your Grace," Pepita went on, "and as my brother-in-law found, there is no power on earth so insuperable or so irresistible."

Once again she realised she had surprised the Duke.

As if she had also made him feel somewhat embarrassed, he rose to his feet to say:

"That is the sentimental maundering of a woman and should not concern men!"

"And yet all through history men have fought and died for love," Pepita answered. "If you look back at your own ancestors, Your Grace, you will find that while they did many great deeds of valour, when they were not on a battlefield they were deeply concerned with love."

The Duke was silent and she was sure he was trying to find the right answer. Then she said:

"I know you do not wish to speak of Alistair, but I would like you to know not only that he had a deep affection for you, but in all the time I lived with him I never heard him say one word against you."

She paused before she added:

"But he was always deeply hurt and distressed that you would no longer. . .acknowledge him as one of your. . .family, which in himself he never ceased to be."

Her voice was very moving as she spoke because Pepita had been so very fond of her brother-in-law, and she was finding it hard to keep the tears from her eyes and from her voice.

Then she added with an effort:

"He talked to Rory about you and about the Castle, so the little boy is not in the least afraid of anything you might do to him."

She waited for the Duke to speak, and when he did not do so, she continued:

"He is waiting now, hoping you will take him fishing with you because he feels instinctively that you, as his grandfather, will take the. . .place of the father he has. . .lost."

All the time she was speaking she was praying that the Duke would understand what she was trying to say to him, and several tears escaped from her eyes and ran down her cheeks.

Hastily she brushed them away, but not before the Duke had seen them.

He walked away to stand at the window with his back to her, looking out to the sea.

She waited, feeling as if she had done everything she could and that if she had failed there was nothing more she could do.

Then he asked:

"Are you prepared to stay here and look after the children, as I understand you have been doing up until now?"

Pepita felt her heart leap, but at first she was afraid she had not heard aright what he had said.

Then in a voice that trembled she replied:

"That is what I have been. . .praying you would. . . allow me to. . .do!"

"Then for the moment we will leave things as they are," the Duke said. "When it becomes clearer what would be best for my grandchildren, we will discuss it again."

Pepita drew in her breath.

"Thank you. . .thank you. . .very much. . .Your Grace."

"Now I am going fishing," the Duke said. "Young Rory had better come with me. It will keep him out of mischief!"

He went from the Study and for a moment it was impossible for Pepita to move.

Then she jumped to her feet and hurried after the Duke, wondering as she did so where Rory would be.

She need not have worried, for the Duke had already gone down the stairs and she could hear his voice in the Hall.

"His Lordship will want some boots," he was saying to Fergus, and the Butler replied:

"Mrs. Sutherland's been a-looking in her cupboards for what his father wore when he was that age, Your Grace, and there are two pairs here which'll fit His Lordship."

"I shall want a rod, Grandpapa," Rory interrupted. "It will have to be longer than the one I had at home, because trout are much smaller than salmon, are they not, Grandpapa?"

Pepita smiled. Then, because she could not see for the tears in her eyes, she turned and went to find Jeanie.

She was quite certain that the men could manage without her and she felt at the moment as if she had fought a battle that had left her victorious but in a state of exhaustion.

*　　*　　*

There was so much to see in the Castle, and the garden in the September sunshine was such an unexpected delight, that the hours seemed to slip by and it was luncheon-time long before she was aware of it.

It was depressing to find that she and Jeanie were alone with the Duchess, who was looking, Pepita thought, plainer and more disagreeable by daylight than she had looked the evening before.

When they appeared, she made no effort to disguise her hostility.

"You are still here, Miss Linford!" she remarked as she and Jeanie came into the Drawing-Room. "I expected by this time you would have packed your boxes and left."

"His Grace has very kindly said that the children can stay," Pepita replied politely.

The Duchess gave what was a scream of anger.

"I do not believe it! I told him I would not have them here and that he was to send them away."

Pepita thought it best not to reply.

She had no wish to antagonise the Duke, and her instinct told her that anything she might say to the Duchess would only make things worse.

Instead she talked to Jeanie, who was occupied in making a fuss of a small spaniel which Pepita realised had been left behind because she was so old.

She had noticed that the Duke always had at his heels two younger spaniels, and she thought that they must be the dogs he took out shooting and knew how delighted Rory would be with them.

Trying to change the subject, she said to Jeanie:

"I think that dog is very old, so you must be very gentle with her."

"She likes me patting her."

"I am sure she does," Pepita agreed.

The Duchess did not speak, and when luncheon was announced she stalked ahead of them disdainfully as if they were beneath her condescension.

Once again it was a delicious meal, and in fact there was so much to eat that Pepita began to think they would all grow very fat.

The Duchess ate in silence, only occasionally speaking to Fergus, who was waiting on them with two footmen to assist him.

Now that she was not so anxious, Pepita could admire

the splendour of the Dining-Room, which was large enough
to seat at least thirty people, and the paintings which hung
on the walls.

They were all of the McNairns and, painted by the
great artists of their time, were not only a very attractive
but a very valuable collection.

Because there was so much she wanted to know about
them, when the Duchess, having finished her luncheon, had
walked out of the room without speaking, she asked Fergus:

"How can I learn all about the Castle? There is so
much I want to know and there are many questions I am
longing to ask."

"That's quite easy, Miss," Fergus replied. "Ye'll find
His Grace's Curator in the Chieftain's Room."

"A Curator?"

"Aye, Miss. He comes here most days, as he's cata-
loguing the contents o' the Castle."

"I would like to talk to him."

"I'm sure he'd be honoured, Miss."

She had found out what she wanted to know, Pepita
thought, but it could keep for later.

It was important now to get Jeanie out in the sunshine.

They went out into the garden and Pepita found at
the far end it was enclosed by a high wall, beyond which
was a rough piece of moorland before the cliffs.

These, rising above the rocks on the shore, stood
higher and more impressive farther along the coast.

She and Jeanie peeped over the edge of the wall.

The tide was out, so the waves were not beating
against the rocks in the same way as in Cornwall.

But Pepita felt that never again would she be able to
look at a rough sea without remembering how her sister and
brother-in-law had been drowned.

Because such memories upset her, she took Jeanie
back into the garden where they played with a ball until it
was nearly tea-time.

Then, just as she was thinking they should go back to the Castle Jeanie's hands and tidy her hair for the next meal, she saw Torquil McNairn coming down the steps which led to the terrace.

She smiled at him as he drew nearer, and he said:

"You and Jeanie are the nicest things I have ever seen here, and certainly no nymph, mermaid, or ghost could look so lovely!"

Pepita laughed.

"That is a very pretty speech which I appreciate!"

The way she spoke made Torquil's eyes twinkle, and he said:

"You sound as if you have been having a somewhat difficult time. I imagine Her Grace has not been over-courteous!"

"I feel that is a remark I should not answer," Pepita replied.

Jeanie had run off, trying to catch a butterfly she she had seen hovering over the flowers, and Torquil's eyes were on Pepita's face, as he said:

"You must be aware that you are far too beautiful for any woman, especially the Duchess, to tolerate in her home!"

"You need not tell me we are not wanted," Pepita replied, "but the Duke has said we can stay, and that is all that matters."

"I knew that."

Pepita looked at him sharply.

"Did His Grace tell you so?"

"There was no need," he answered. "When we met on the river and I saw that Rory was with him, I knew that the call of his blood was stronger than his dislike of the Sassenachs!"

Pepita could not help smiling.

"It seems impossible in this day and age that any man should hate us so violently because of something which happened over a hundred years ago!"

"You will learn that the Scots never forget and that time does not count," Torquil replied. "The battles in which we were involved all happened yesterday, and our grievances do not grow less over the years but intensify."

"It seems foolish and unfair!"

"That is the English point of view."

"What is yours?" Pepita enquired.

"All you need to know," he answered quietly, "is that you are the most beautiful person I have ever seen and that I want to protect you from all the consequences your beauty will cause. I have a feeling your beauty will be far more dangerous than your nationality."

Pepita laughed as if she could not help it.

"Now you are trying to frighten me!" she protested. "I am sure that nobody, not even the Duchess, will be much concerned with the looks of a humble Governess."

Now Torquil laughed.

"Is that what you intend to be?"

"That is what I am! And do help me remember that I must keep my 'place.' "

He laughed again. Then he said quite seriously:

"If things are difficult, if you have problems, will you promise to remember that I want to help you?"

"Thank you," Pepita said. "I have a feeling I may need a friend. At the same time, as a McNairn, you may prove to be an enemy."

"That is an unkind thing to say!" he exclaimed. "If I had any aspirations or ambitions, which actually I have not, I might be opposed to your arrival for the same reasons as the Duchess!"

Pepita looked at him in a puzzled way, and he explained:

"Before the Duke remarried—and actually it was I who suggested he should do so—I was his heir presumptive as Chieftain."

"Are you saying he was going to make you Chieftain of the Clan?"

"After he dismissed Alistair and was resolved that his son should play no further part in his life, the Duke intended to introduce me to the Clan as his successor."

"But. . .you said it was your idea that he should. . .get married."

"As I had no intention of marrying Flora McDonavan," Torquil said, "I suggested to the Duke that it would be much simpler if she gave him the heir he was so determined to have."

Pepita stared at Torquil as if she could hardly believe what she had heard.

Then she said:

"Are you saying that. . .the Duchess was the. . .woman the Duke. . .wished you to marry?"

"She is a McDonavan and actually the only eligible daughter of the present Chieftain."

Pepita put up her hands almost protestingly.

"I. . .I cannot believe it!" she said. "In England we are talking about the Emancipation of Women, and here in Scotland you seem to be living in the Dark Ages!"

"Yet you can see I have escaped!" Torquil said. "But now, thanks to you, all His Grace's plans have been upset."

"You mean since Rory is his heir!"

"Exactly! So you can hardly expect the Duchess to welcome him with open arms."

"She might not have a son!"

"That of course is in the lap of the gods," Torquil replied, "but she is young, and the Duke is magnificent for his age!"

There was silence. Then Pepita said, watching Jeanie still running after the butterfly:

"I can see it must be all very upsetting. At the same time, nothing can be done about it."

"Nothing," Torquil agreed, "unless we drop you all in the sea or lose you on the moors!"

He spoke lightly and Pepita laughed.

"I hope that will not happen."

"I have already promised to look after you."

There was an intense note in Torquil's voice that made her feel shy, and she moved away from him towards Jeanie.

"We must go get ready for tea. Come along, Jeanie, and if you want to try to catch a butterfly, I will buy you a net like the one I used to have when I was a little girl."

"Which was not so very long ago!" Torquil remarked.

She walked towards the child and he walked close beside her.

It suddenly struck her that the Duke and certainly the Duchess might think it very reprehensible if they thought she was flirting with a young man as soon as she had arrived at the Castle.

She therefore caught Jeanie by the hand and, despite the child's protests, hurried her up the steps from the garden, acutely aware that all the time Torquil was following them.

She could hear his footsteps, and at the same time she felt that he was somehow encroaching on her and it was difficult to escape from him.

'I must be careful,' she thought, 'very, very careful. If I annoy the Duke, he might change his mind and not allow me to stay with the children.'

At the same time, she could not help thinking how strange it was that he had planned that Torquil should be the next Chieftain.

"How could he completely ignore Alistair?" she asked herself indignantly.

As they went upstairs she appreciated the luxury of the Castle, the paintings, the furniture, and the numbers of servants to wait on them.

She did not have to tidy Jeanie's hair when they reached their bedrooms since there was a housemaid waiting to do it for her.

She only had to see to herself.

There was no sign of Rory, and when she and Jeanie went into the Breakfast-Room, where tea was laid, they found the Duchess and Torquil sitting at the large round table.

It was laden with every sort of delicacy, including scones, baps, bannocks and griddle-cakes, freshly baked bread, half-a-dozen home-made jams, ginger snaps, and a huge fruit-cake which Pepita was certain would prove very indigestible.

The Duchess did not speak when they came into the room, but Fergus brought Pepita a cup of tea, which he poured out for her, and placed a glass of milk beside Jeanie.

There was a rather uncomfortable silence until the child said:

"I nearly caught a butterfly! Tomorrow I will catch lots of butterflies and put them in a jar and watch their wings flutter."

"If you do that, they will die," Torquil said.

Jeanie shook her head.

"No. Mama said after I had watched them I must let them fly away, otherwise it would be cruel."

"That is the right thing to do," Torquil agreed. "Butterflies are very fragile and pretty, in fact they look like you as you were running about the garden!"

"I's too big to be a butterfly!" Jeanie said in practical tones.

"Really, Torquil!" the Duchess interposed. "Do we have to have this ridiculous nursery conversation at every meal? I shall tell my husband that in future the children must eat in the School-Room, which is the right place for them."

Torquil did not answer. He merely looked at Pepita, then passed his cup to the Duchess, saying:

"May I have another cup of tea? I find that fishing makes me thirsty."

The Duchess did not reply but started to pour tea into his cup.

"In case you are interested," he added, "I caught three salmon today, and one of them weighed over twelve pounds."

Pepita found it impossible to repress a little cry of excitement.

"May I see them?" she asked. "I have always wanted to see a salmon when it first comes out of the river."

Before Torquil could reply, the Duchess said sharply:

"I think Miss Linford, you should confine yourself to teaching the children, which is what I understand you are here to do. The sport of His Grace or his guests is no concern of yours."

"I apologise, Your Grace," Pepita said quickly, "but I find both the sport and the customs of this strange and extraordinarily backward country very interesting from an academic point of view!"

For a moment she realised that the Duchess did not understand what she meant, but she was aware that Torquil was having difficulty in repressing his laughter.

Then the Duchess rose to her feet to leave the room in what would have been a dignified manner if she had not been so ungainly.

Only when she was out of earshot did Torquil say:

"That was a hard ball straight at the middle stump! At the same time, you are facing a very implacable enemy!"

"She is determined to make that clear," Pepita replied. "Ever since I arrived she has done nothing but tell me we must leave immediately because we are not wanted!"

"I do not think the Duke will listen to her," Torquil said, "but I think she will make trouble for you if she can."

"I am much more worried about the children. It is bad for them to hear people bickering over their heads, which is something they have never been used to."

"If your sister was as lovely as you," Torquil remarked, "I can understand Alistair thinking Scotland was no loss."

"He very much minded losing Scotland," Pepita replied, "but love is a gift from Heaven."

She gave a little sigh before she went on:

"You may not believe it, but if I had the choice I would not hesitate to exchange this marvellous Castle for the small house in which we lived in Cornwall. We were very poor, but it always seemed to be filled with sunshine and laughter."

"That is what you have brought here," Torquil said.

Their eyes met across the table and Pepita felt it was hard to look away.

Then, before she could speak, a wildly excited Rory came rushing into the room.

"I have caught a salmon, a great big one!" he cried. "Come see it, please, Aunt Pepita, come see it!"

"I would love to do that," Pepita replied.

Then when she rose to her feet she saw that the Duke had joined them.

"I think you had better have your tea first," he said to Rory, "and when the gillies have laid all the fish out on a slab, we will go down and admire them."

He spoke in such a gentle tone that Pepita stared at him before she asked:

"Did Rory really catch a salmon?"

The Duke smiled.

"Shall we say that he had a little help, especially in bringing it in for the gaff."

"It is the biggest fish you have ever seen, Aunt Pepita!" Rory cried. "Bigger than me, and I was very clever to catch it!"

Torquil laughed and said to the Duke:

"I know exactly what he is feeling! That is just how I felt when I caught my first salmon, but I was two years older than he is!"

The Duke sat down at the opposite end of the table from where the tea-things were laid out, looked at Pepita, and said:

"I suggest, Miss Linford, as my wife is not here, that you pour me a cup of tea. Fergus is fetching Rory another pair of stockings, as his are wet."

"The river went right over the top of my boots, Aunt Pepita," Rory said proudly, "but I did not fall in!"

"I am glad about that," Pepita replied.

She sat down in the place the Duchess had vacated and poured out a cup of tea for the Duke, which Torquil passed to him.

When she had done so, he gave her his cup, and she was filling it when the door opened and the Duchess came into the room.

"I heard you were back, Kelvin. . ." she began, then saw Pepita sitting in her place.

She walked towards her, her face contorted with rage as she exclaimed:

"How dare you! How dare you assume the position as hostess at my table and in my house!"

"I. . .I am sorry. . ." Pepita said, and began rising from the chair, but the Duke interrupted:

"Do not be ridiculous, Flora! I asked Miss Linford to pour me a cup of tea as you were not here."

Pepita had moved away but the Duchess stood at the table staring at her husband.

"I will not have that woman here! Do you understand? She is to leave now, immediately, tonight! She is not only English, but already she is behaving like a harlot. I saw her out my window flirting with Torquil on the lawn in a way no decent woman would behave!"

The words seemed to pour out of the Duchess's mouth with an uncontrollable venom that was frightening.

Then as Pepita drew in her breath and wondered if

she should run away before she heard any more, the Duke said in a voice of thunder:

"That is enough, Flora! You are upsetting yourself quite unnecessarily! Go to your room and lie down!"

It was an order that sounded almost like a cannon-shot.

In the passing of a second the Duchess stared at her husband as if she would defy him. Then she burst into tears and went from the room.

For a moment there was an awkward silence, until Rory, who had his mouth full of hot scone, asked:

"Why is she unhappy? Would she like to see my salmon."

Because it was so ridiculous, Pepita felt she wanted to laugh. Then, as if he would somehow disperse the awkwardness they all were feeling, the Duke said:

"Hurry up and eat your tea and we will go to see the salmon."

Jeanie, feeling she had been neglected, rose from her seat to stand at the Duke's side.

"Rory caught a salmon," she said, "but I nearly caught a butterfly! It was a very pretty one!"

"You must tell me about it," the Duke said.

"That man," Jeanie went on, pointing to Torquil, "said that I looked like a butterfly, but he is silly! I's too big to be a butterfly!"

"Much too big," the Duke agreed, "but not much bigger than Rory's salmon!"

Pepita listened to this exchange in amazement.

Then she felt her heart singing.

Mr. Clarence had been right. The children had inherited their father's magnetic charm, and the Duke was captivated.

Chapter Four

The ladies came out of the Dining-Room, and Pepita, who came last, thought she would slip away.

As usual the Duchess had ignored her and deliberately had not introduced her to the guests at dinner.

Some of them were staying in the house, but the rest had seemed somewhat astonished when the Duchess made no effort to explain who Pepita was.

It was left to Torquil, who as usual was pouring oil on troubled waters, who said to an elderly and obviously important lady:

"I do not think you have met Alistair's sister-in-law, who brought his children here after he died."

Instantly there was a look of interest and curiosity in the Dowager's eyes, and after that everybody in the party whom Pepita had not met already wanted to talk to her.

She thought the way in which they spoke so warmly of Alistair was very touching, and it was obvious that they had not forgotten him.

But she realised that every word that was said to her infuriated the Duchess, and this made her feel uncomfortable.

Every day, it seemed to her, the Duchess's antagonism increased not only towards her but towards the children.

She never spoke to them except to find fault, and when possible she swept by them disdainfully as if they were beneath her condescension.

Now Pepita thought that as it was growing late, it would be more comfortable for her to disappear rather than to sit in the Drawing-Room, conscious of the Duchess's hatred vibrating towards her whether she spoke or kept silent.

She therefore decided to go to bed, and started to walk down the passage towards her own room and the Sitting-Room next to it, which had now been allotted to the children.

It was there that she had begun to give them their lessons, finding it a hard thing to do where Rory was concerned.

If his grandfather was fishing he wished to fish with him, and the Duke had already allowed the small boy to go with him when shooting on the moors, although he had not yet allowed him to carry a gun.

It was obvious to Pepita that the Duke was delighted with Rory and also found it hard to resist Jeanie.

At the same time, she knew that where she was concerned there was an unbreakable barrier between them.

She had almost reached her bedroom when at the end of the passage she saw the moonlight shining through an uncurtained window.

She then decided that it was a perfect night to go to the Watch-Tower.

It was Mrs. Sutherland who had told her originally that there was "a grand view" from the Watch-Tower, and when Rory was out with the Duke she and Jeanie had climbed the twisting stairs of the old Tower and gone onto the flat roof.

In the old days she knew there had always been a Clansman stationed there to watch for the approach of Vikings, or scanning the moors for the first sight of hostile Clansmen, who were usually the McDonavans.

Mrs. Sutherland had been right.

The view was indeed fantastic, and Pepita felt she needed beauty to take away the feeling of depression which contact with the Duchess always gave her.

She therefore pulled open the door which led to the Tower and started to climb the twisting stone steps, seeing her way by the moonlight coming through the ancient arrow-slits.

When she opened the door at the top, the moon seemed almost dazzling in its brightness as she stepped out onto the roof.

If the view had been beautiful in the sunshine with its strange lights on the moors and a shimmering haze over the sea, the moonlight made it even more spectacular.

The moon was almost full and the stars in the sky seemed more brilliant than any Pepita had ever seen before.

The gardens were touched with silver, as was the sea beyond them, and she felt as if she had walked into a fairy-land and that everything commonplace and ugly was left behind.

Because beauty always moved her, she felt as if her whole being leapt towards the wonder and magic of it and it became part of herself.

Then suddenly—and somehow it did not seem an intrusion, but almost as if she had expected it to happen—she heard a deep voice behind her say:

"I thought this was where I would find you!"

"I could not believe anything could be so lovely!" she exclaimed.

"That is what I thought when I first saw you."

For a moment it did not seem to matter that he should be paying her a compliment, nor did she remember that she had been trying for the last few days to avoid being alone with him.

Then he said very quietly:

"You know, Pepita, that I love you!"

The depth of his voice and the sincere way in which he spoke seemed for a moment to hypnotise her. Then with a little cry she came back to reality.

"No. . .no. . .you must not say. . .such a. . .thing!"

"Why not?" he asked. "It is true that I love you, and there is nothing in life I want more than that you should marry me!"

It was then that she turned to look up at him, her eyes very wide and frightened in her face.

"Are you. . .crazy?"

"Yes," he replied, "so crazy that I can no longer go on as we are."

He put his arms round her as he spoke, and before she could resist him, before she could put up her hands to defend herself, his lips were on hers.

For a second she was too surprised to move, and when she tried to, it was too late.

His lips were hard and compelling, and even as it flashed through her mind that she must escape from him, she knew she had no wish to do so.

Something warm and wonderful moved through her breast and up her throat to touch her lips.

Then as his kiss became more demanding, more possessive, she felt as if the moonlight seeped through her body and the beauty of it gave her a sensation she had never felt before.

It was so wonderful, so glorious that it seemed not real but part of the magic that had been in her dreams, and yet suddenly it was hers.

Torquil held her closer and still closer, until, when she felt as if he had given her not only the light of the moon but the stars shimmering in her breast, he raised his head.

"I love you, I adore you!" he said. "Nothing shall stop me from making you my wife!"

He spoke with fierce determination, and when she tried to tell him it was impossible, his lips were on hers again.

He kissed her fiercely, demandingly, compellingly, in a way which told her that he was afraid of losing her.

Caught up once again with the magic that made it impossible to think, she could only feel the moonlight rippling through her until it became a rapture beyond words, and at the same time almost a pain.

She could only surrender herself to the wonder of it.

Then at last, as if the ecstasy of their feelings made it imperative to breathe, Pepita gave a little murmur and hid her face against Torquil's neck.

"I love you!" he said, and his voice was deep and unsteady. "God, how I love you!"

She did not answer. She could find no words in which to do so.

Very gently he put his fingers under her chin and turned her face up to his.

"Tell me what you feel about me."

"I. . .love you. . .too," she whispered, "but. . .I did not know that love was. . .like this."

"Like what, my precious?"

"So wonderful that I feel I am no longer on earth but floating amongst the. . .stars."

"That is how I feel too," he said. "My darling, you have made it very difficult for me these last few days. I realised you were trying to avoid me, when all I wanted was that we should acknowledge the love we have for each other."

"It is. . .something we. . .must not do."

"Why not?"

She gave a sigh that seemed to come from the very depths of her being.

"You. . .know why."

"The only thing I know," he replied harshly, "is that I want you, and because I know you love me, my beautiful one, nothing else is of any importance."

With an almost superhuman effort Pepita managed to move a little away from him, even though his arms were still round her.

"Listen to me," she said, "please. . .you must listen to me."

"I am listening," he answered, "but you know that all I want to do is kiss you."

She pressed both her hands hard against his chest to prevent him from doing so, then she said:

"The children. . .I have to. . .think of the. . .children!"

Torquil did not answer, and after a moment she went on:

"You know that if the Duke realises what we feel for each other he will send me away. . .and I cannot leave the children here without anybody to. . .protect them."

"Protect them?" Torquil asked. "You are not really afraid of the Duchess!"

"She hates them!" Pepita replied. "She is trying to turn the Duke. . .against them, even though she has. . . failed up to. . .now."

"But he is fond of them, and he would see that they came to no harm."

"You know I cannot. . .leave them."

"You cannot stay here for the rest of your life," Torquil said harshly, "being treated as an outcast and enduring incredible rudeness from that damned woman!"

He spoke violently, and because it was unexpected it made Pepita smile.

"You are. . .supposed," she said a little unsteadily, "to have. . .made up your feud with the. . .McDonavans."

"If they were all like the Duchess," Torquil replied, "I would exterminate the whole Clan, if it were within my power to do so!"

He pulled her back into his arms again and said:

"Neither the McDonavans nor anyone else can prevent us from being together."

He would have kissed her, but Pepita turned her face away from him so that his lips rested on her cheek as she said:

"I am not only. . .thinking of the. . .children, but also of. . .you."

"Of me?" he questioned. "In what way?"

"You are a McNairn, and I know the Duke loves you and treats you as if you were his son. He exiled his real son because he married my sister; what do you think he would do to you if he knew that you loved me?"

"He is not my father."

"No, but he is your Chieftain," Pepita replied, "and you know as well as I do that although you are independent of him, your lands march with his, and you are a McNairn and part of the Clan."

"I am not afraid of him," Torquil said, "and the only thing that matters to me is you. You fill my whole life and I cannot think of anything but you and your beauty."

Pepita gave a deep sigh.

"Please. . .please be. . .sensible," she begged, "for your own sake as well as for mine!"

"And what do you call 'sensible'?"

"I think it would be best if you went away, at least for a while," she replied, "until we can forget what has happened tonight."

His arms tightened round her.

"Will you forget?"

"That is. . .different."

"Why is it different?"

She would have hidden her face against him, but once again he turned it up to his.

"Answer me truthfully," he said. "Will you forget my love, and that I have kissed you?"

Her eyes fell before his and she could not answer.

Then once again his lips were on hers and he kissed her violently, fiercely, and so possessively that she felt as if she became a part of him and no longer had any identity of her own.

Then as if the softness and sweetness of her lips made him aware of how vulnerable she was, his kisses became more tender and gentle, and she felt as if he wooed her in a manner that was impossible to resist, impossible to deny.

She knew as he kissed her that she had loved him from the first moment when she had felt he was the only friend she had in the Castle.

It had grown every day as she saw him looking so incredibly handsome in his kilt. She had fallen more and more in love with him until she could not think of anybody else when he was there and she dreamt of him every night.

Now at this moment as she surrendered herself to the ecstasy he evoked in her, she knew that this was love as she had always wanted to find it.

It was the love her sister had had for Alistair and he for her.

It was the love that had always been in her dreams and which she had hoped she might one day find if she was very, very lucky.

Now she had found it, but because it was love for a man to whom she must never mean anything, she had to be strong and refuse it.

Almost as if he could read her thoughts and knew what she was feeling, Torquil raised his head and said:

"What can we do, my precious love?"

Then before she could reply he said:

"I intend to marry you, but I understand what you feel about the children."

"How can I. . .trust the. . .Duke?" Pepita asked.

Her voice was very low and it was difficult to speak because Torquil was kissing her cheek and her heart was beating frantically against his.

"I know that the way he behaved towards Alistair was abominable and unnatural," Torquil replied, "but perhaps now he has learnt his lesson."

"How can you be sure of that?" Pepita asked. "And there is the. . .Duchess."

"I do not believe that she could now persuade him to send them away."

"But. . .if she has a son," Pepita said, "she will hate Rory more than she does already, and she might even. . . harm him."

"That is ridiculous!" Torquil protested. "I agree she would want her own son to be in his place, but even so you cannot protect him forever, and soon he will have to go to School."

"The Duke may. . .send them both away."

"I am sure he will not do that."

"I am not. . .sure of. . .anything," Pepita said desperately.

"Except of me! You must be sure, my darling, that I love you, and sure too that sooner or later, although we may have to wait, you will be my wife."

"What sort of life would it be for you. . .exiled by the Duke from your kith and kin. . .with the members of the Clan. . .hating me as I am sure they hated my sister."

Torquil was silent and she knew he could not in all sincerity contradict what she had said.

Very gently she moved from his arms.

"You must go back," she said. "The Duke may. . .miss you and. . .suspect that you are with. . .me."

"They will be playing Bridge and I shall not be missed," Torquil replied.

"How can you be sure of that. . .or of anything else?" Pepita asked. "Oh, Torquil, I am. . .afraid!"

"My precious, my darling, I have no wish to make things more difficult for you than they are already," he said, "but I love you so desperately, and I cannot lose you."

Pepita walked a few steps to the edge of the Tower and looked out over the sea.

Her whole being was throbbing with the wonder Torquil had evoked in her.

For the moment it was difficult to think that it was wrong of him to have kissed her and that his love was something she should refuse.

She needed him, and while every nerve in her body vibrated towards him, she knew he felt the same.

He moved to stand beside her. Then he said:

"We will always remember this moment because it means so much to both of us, and I swear to you by everything in which I believe that you will be mine and we will be together, whatever the odds against us."

The way he spoke was very moving, and Pepita turned her head to look at him. Then as their eyes met it was impossible to look away.

"Tell me," Torquil said, "as you stand here and we have left the world behind, what you feel about me."

"I. . .love you!" Pepita said very softly.

"And I love you!"

She knew it was a vow they were making which was something so sacred to them both that neither of them could ever break it.

Then he said:

"As I love, adore, and worship you, my darling, so will I move Heaven and earth if necessary to make you mine. In the meantime, I will be very careful not to do anything that would hurt you."

He took her hand in his and raised it to his lips.

Then as she felt his kiss on the softness of her skin, a little quiver ran through her, and he said:

"Take care of yourself, my lovely wife-to-be. Dream of me and pray that as God has brought us together He will give us to each other, because otherwise neither of us will ever find happiness."

He kissed her hand again, then turning he walked away and disappeared through the darkness of the Tower door and she heard his footsteps going slowly down the twisting stone stairs.

Only when she could hear him no longer did she put her hands over her eyes and feel as if her whole body was throbbing with the glory of a love that was beyond anything she had ever dreamt or imagined.

This was not only beauty, the beauty of music and flowers, the stars and the moon, it was also a very human need for a man!

Torquil, she thought, was everything a man should be: idealistic, kind, and generous, and at the same time determined and authoritative in the things that mattered.

At this moment it was not hard to believe that only by some miracle would she be able to become his wife.

"I love him, I love him!" Pepita whispered.

Then, as if she was suddenly aware of the enormity of the difficulties that lay ahead of them, she lifted up her arms to the stars overhead, and with an intensity which came from her very soul she prayed:

"Help me. . .please, God. . .help me! Do not let me. . .lose anything so wonderful. . .help us to find. . .a way in which we can be together. . ."

She prayed aloud, but her voice seemed lost in the stillness of the night.

Then, as if the shimmering moonlight on the sea had

lost some of its power to entrance her, Pepita turned and very slowly left the Tower.

Shutting out the wonder of the night, she crept quietly down the stairs towards her bedroom.

* * *

The next day the guests who had been staying at the Castle went off early after breakfast to shoot on the moors, and Rory went with them.

Torquil was not at breakfast, and Pepita knew that it was because after what they had said and felt last night he could not face her when there were so many other people present.

Rory was excited about going out with his grandfather, and all through breakfast he kept asking him:

"When can I shoot, Grandpapa? You promised me I could, and I want to shoot just as well as you do."

"That is a compliment, Duke," one of the older guests laughed. "In a year or two, like all young people today, he will be saying that he shoots better than you do."

"I have a few years left," the Duke answered in a good-humoured voice.

As if she thought Rory was having too much attention, Jeanie got down from her chair and walked to her grandfather's side.

"I want to come with you, Grandpapa," she said. "I would like to shoot, too."

The Duke took her up onto his knee.

"Ladies do not shoot," he said firmly.

"Then I am the exception, Kelvin," the Duchess said from the end of the table. "I may inform you that I am an extremely good shot with both a rifle and a gun!"

She spoke in a hard, rather aggressive voice that made some of the guests look at her in surprise.

When the Duke did not answer, she went on:

"My husband is old-fashioned enough to think that women should confine themselves to sewing and knitting, but I have always been able to fish as well as my brothers, shoot as well as they can, if not better, and certainly beat them when it comes to riding!"

The way she was boasting told Pepita that she wished to draw attention to herself and was once again annoyed at the Duke's attitude towards his grandchildren.

"I am sorry to tell you, Duchess, that I too do not like to see women shooting," one of the other guests remarked. "Like Kelvin, I am old-fashioned."

"When you come to stay with us next year," the Duchess replied, "expect to find me on the moors beside you, and I shall be able to prove my point that a woman can often be the equal of a man, even in what you consider is essentially a man's sport."

The Duke rose abruptly from the other end of the table.

"We will be leaving in five minutes!" he said sharply. "Hurry up and get ready, Rory, or I shall go without you!"

Rory gave a cry of horror at the idea and ran from the room, and Pepita hastily followed him.

Jeanie held on to her grandfather's hand.

"When you come back, Grandpapa," she said, "will you bring me a piece of white heather to bring me luck? You must pick it yourself, 'cause Fergus says that a piece of white heather from the Chieftain of the McNairns is the luckiest charm anybody could own."

Several of the Duke's guests laughed, and one of them said:

"I am sure you could not refuse such a request, Kelvin, even though most of the 'Charmers' you have pursued in the past would have demanded orchids."

Then, as if he felt he had been indiscreet because the Duchess was present, he added:

"I must hurry, or I shall keep you waiting, and I have

no wish to commit the unforgivable sin of delaying the guns!"

Jeanie was still waiting for an answer, and the Duke looked down at her from his great height and said:

"I will try to find you a piece of white heather. If not, I will bring you a feather for you to tuck into your bonnet."

"I would like both, Grandpapa," Jeanie said.

Again the Duke's guests were teasing him as they left the Dining-Room and went down the stairs.

The Duchess did not move from her place at the end of the table, but there was an expression on her plain face which would have frightened Pepita had she seen it.

Jeanie had some lessons in the morning, then Pepita took her out for a walk before luncheon, going through the garden gate and across the rough land at the edge of the cliffs.

There were some twisting steps cut into the rock so that people from the Castle could descend quite easily onto the beach below.

But because the tide was in and the waves would have splashed them, Pepita would not allow Jeanie to climb down.

"We will do it when the tide is out," she said, "then we will look for shells. I remember your father saying that when he was a small boy he used to find some very pretty shells on the beach."

"I want to find them," Jeanie said.

"We will find lots," Pepita replied, "and then I will make you a necklace of them."

"That would be lovely!" Jeanie replied.

She danced with excitement along the edge of the cliff, but Pepita caught hold of her.

"You must not go too near the edge, darling," she said. "Cliffs are always dangerous."

Then, knowing it was growing close to luncheon-time, she took Jeanie back to the Castle.

Nothing much happened in the afternoon, but teatime, with so many people staying in the Castle and other guests invited, could have been interesting if Pepita had not constantly been aware of the Duchess's animosity.

She had the feeling, although she knew it might have been her imagination, that this was growing in intensity, and she thought that when the Duchess looked at her, which was not often, she was wishing her dead.

"I am being imaginative," she told herself.

At the same time, her instinct told her that the Duchess's hatred was so violent and so intense that it was almost as if she were encountering a wild beast.

'It is very bad for the Duchess to feel like this when she is carrying a child,' she thought to herself.

She remembered her sister saying that when Rory and Jeanie were on the way, she tried always to think beautiful thoughts and never to be disagreeable because it might affect her unborn child.

"That is what the Greeks believed," Denise had said, "and I am sure they were right. We form our children's characters long before they are born, and I am determined my children will be everything that is fine, gallant, and loving, just like their father."

She had smiled at Alistair as she spoke, and he had replied:

"Just like you, my darling, and who could be more adorable in every way?"

As they looked at each other they had forgotten that Pepita was there, and as her sister turned to whisper something to her husband, Pepita slipped from the room, thinking it was impossible for two people to be any happier.

Their joy at being with each other seemed to light the whole house with a sunshine that came from within themselves rather than from the sky above them.

"That is what I want to feel," Pepita told herself.

She knew now there was only one man who could

make her feel like that, the man she had been conscious of ever since she had arrived in Scotland.

Only to look at Torquil sitting at the other end of the table made her heart seem to turn strange somersaults in her breast.

She had looked away from him because she knew that love was something that was unmistakably revealed in the eyes, and if anybody intercepted a look between them, they would be well aware what they both were feeling.

After dinner that evening Pepita had a strong impulse to go to the Watch-Tower again. Then she knew it would be the wrong thing to do.

"I must think of Torquil," she told herself. "If I am sent away by the Duke, I would somehow survive, but for him it would destroy his whole way of life as he knows it."

She had learnt from Mrs. Sutherland, who was an inveterate gossip, that Torquil's Castle was very beautiful and very much older than the Duke's.

It had been built as a stronghold by the McNairns and had more than once resisted an onslaught by the Vikings, besides sieges from another warring Clan.

"Does Mr. Torquil live there by himself?" Pepita had asked curiously.

"Since his mother died Mr. Torquil's been here more than he's been at home," Mrs. Sutherland answered. "His Grace has come to rely on him, having no son to help him in his old age."

Pepita bit back the words that that was his own fault, but because she was curious she enquired:

"And Mr. Torquil has no brothers or sisters?"

Mrs. Sutherland shook her head.

"His younger brother was killed when he was in the Army, an' it were awfu' sad, for his father had no other sons. I've often said to Mr. Torquil: 'Get ye'sel' a wife, mon, and hae a dozen bairns to fill the Castle an' make it a real hame.'"

"What was Mr. Torquil's reply to that?"

Mrs. Sutherland laughed.

"Like all men, he's waiting for the right woman to come alang, an' one day he'll find her."

To Pepita her words were like a sharp pain in her breast.

Torquil might think she was the right woman, but how could she fill the Castle with children when they would be ostracised and hated as Alistair had been when he was driven away from his home and from everything that was familiar?

"I love Torquil too much to do that to him," Pepita whispered.

So after dinner she did not leave the Drawing-Room, but sat talking to Lady Rogart, one of the elderly guests who did not play Bridge and who said that she found her eyes were too weak to read at night by the oil-lamps with which the Drawing-Room was lit.

She, like Mrs. Sutherland, was also a gossip, but Pepita was very careful not to speak of Torquil.

Instead she answered quite simply her questions about Alistair and told her how happy he had been, despite the fact that he sorely missed Scotland and his own people.

"We McNairns have all been very curious about him, as you can imagine," Lady Rogart said.

As the Duchess had not introduced her to anybody, it had taken Pepita some time to find out who the guests were.

Then she realised that Lady Rogart had been a McNairn before she married.

A little tentatively Pepita said:

"I have often wondered why none of the McNairn relations ever got in touch with Alistair. I think he would have been delighted to hear from them."

"For one thing," Lady Rogart replied, "we had no idea where he was, and secondly I think the male McNairns, at any rate, were afraid of offending the Duke."

She gave a little laugh and added:

"The Scots are a very practical people, Miss Linford, and as the Duke has the best shooting anywhere in Scotland, none of them was anxious to be on his 'Black List'!"

Pepita laughed because it was such a simple answer to a complex question.

At the same time, she still thought it cruel that Alistair had been cut off all those years without a kind word from even one of his relatives, and she knew she could not allow that to happen to the man she loved.

'I must go away,' she thought despairingly.

When she went to bed she knew there was no other solution.

Once she could trust the Duke to look after the children and not to allow the Duchess to say or do anything to harm them, she would have to find herself another place to live.

This meant of course that she must also find some employment, since she had no money and no chance of ever having any except what she could earn by the few talents she possessed.

'What can I do?' she thought frantically, and knew the real answer was that jobs for somebody like herself were almost nonexistent.

She could, however, be a Governess, as she was at the moment to her nephew and niece, but at the same time she was practical enough to realise that few women would want to accept in their homes a Governess who looked like her.

It was not conceit to realise that she and Denise had both taken after their mother, who had been outstandingly beautiful.

Also, she had not missed since she had arrived at the Castle the looks of startled surprise that came into the eyes of the lady guests when they saw her, or the looks of admiration she received from the men.

Apart from teaching children, she supposed she could be a companion to some elderly and doubtless cantankerous old woman.

It was not a very happy prospect, and she knew all the time she was thinking out the alternatives that her heart was crying out in agony at the thought of having to say good-bye to Torquil.

There was something about him which drew her irresistibly, and she knew he had been right when he had said that they belonged to each other.

She was really incredibly lucky, she thought, to have found, out of the whole world, the one man whom God had meant to be the other part of herself.

She could think of nothing more perfect than to be his wife, to love him, to look after him, and to bear his children.

Then she knew that this was just a dream, and whatever Torquil might say it could never come true.

How could she ask him to suffer the poverty that Alistair had suffered, or to endure the isolation which, now that she looked back on it, had been something that most men would have found intolerable?

"Torquil has no idea what it means to be ostracised and suddenly alone in the world," she told herself.

She knew that Alistair would never have done anything other than to marry her sister.

But she felt she could never live with Torquil without always being afraid that one day he would regret having cut himself off from everything which had filled his life until now.

In the first place, he was older than Alistair had been when he had believed the world was well lost for love.

Even more important, since he owned his own Castle and his own Estate, it would probably be even more difficult for him to take such a far-reaching step than it had been for Alistair, who had always lived under the shadow of the Duke and had never really known independence.

"I cannot do it to him," Pepita whispered into her pillow. "I love him too much."

At the same time, she had no idea what she should do or what would happen to her in the future either if she stayed on or if she went away.

"How can I remain here, loving and wanting him," she argued with herself, "and knowing we are in danger of discovery every time we meet?"

Alternatively, she knew that to leave was to risk starvation and perhaps to be forced to take employment that would have shocked and upset her father.

'If only Papa could have made friends in England, as well as all over the world,' she thought, 'it would be easier.'

She could remember his speaking of some charming people he had known in Spain, which was where she had been born and which was why she had a Spanish name.

He also had a number of friends in France and Italy.

But even if she got in touch with them she could hardly at the same time ask them to send her enough money to travel out to meet them.

Then it occurred to her that it was possible that they might be able to offer her employment as a teacher of English.

The only qualification she had for this was that she could speak French fluently, and if she studied hard she could improve both her Spanish and her Italian.

At the same time, even to think of going off alone to strange countries was so frightening that it was difficult to contemplate taking such a step.

Her father had retired from the Foreign Office when she was nine and Denise was sixteen, and after that they had lived in England.

Looking back, it was difficult to remember much about the countries in which they had lived and the people whom her father and mother had known there.

"I must concentrate on England," she told herself. "There must be some Linford relations somewhere!"

She knew that her father's elder sister, who had been much older and had lived in Bath, was now dead.

His other sister, who had married a rich man, had, after she had been widowed, moved to the South of France, and because she was perpetually ill and her eye-sight had deteriorated she had not cummunicated with either Denise or herself after their father's death.

"She may still be alive, or she may not," Pepita reasoned. "Anyway, I am sure by this time she would be too old or too ill to want me."

This brought her back to the question she had asked herself when she got into bed.

"What am I to do?"

Now it seemed almost to be whispered down the high-ceilinged room in which she was sleeping.

"What shall I do? What shall I do?"

She could hear the same words on the wind outside and thought they were echoed by the murmur of the waves in the far distance.

"What can I do?"

It was a cry of despair.

Then, because he was always on the edge of her thoughts and in every beat of her heart, she felt as if Torquil put his arms round her and held her close against him.

'I have to forget him!' she thought despairingly.

But she knew she would never cease to think of him and to love him, and would know that while she was yearning for him, he at the same time was yearning for her.

Chapter Five

As luncheon finished, the two elderly lady guests told the Duchess they were going into the garden.

"Yes, do that," the Duchess replied, "and I will join you later."

She then turned to Pepita and Jeanie, who were following them, and said in a harsh voice:

"I want to speak to you, Miss Linford."

"I will take Jeanie to Mrs. Sutherland, Your Grace," Pepita replied, "and then I will come to the Drawing-Room."

The Duchess did not reply. She merely walked ahead with the usual disdainful air which she always assumed when she was speaking to the children or Pepita.

Wondering what the Duchess could have to say to her, Pepita hurried Jeanie down the passage to the Housekeeper's room.

"I want to go out in the garden, Aunt Pepita!" Jeanie cried.

"We will do that in a few minutes," Pepita answered.

"I want to go now!" the child protested.

Pepita promised that she would not be long, and when she reached the Housekeeper's room she was relieved to find that Mrs. Sutherland was there.

"Will you look after Her Ladyship for a few minutes, Mrs. Sutherland?" she asked. "Her Grace wants me."

She thought there was an apprehensive look on the Housekeeper's face, but she did not say anything and held out her hand towards Jeanie.

"I've something verry exciting to show tae Yer Ladyship," she said ingratiatingly.

"What is it?" Jeanie enquired.

"Two wee kittens born just last night."

Pepita did not need to listen to any more. She was sure that Jeanie would be enthralled and quite happy until she returned.

She knew she must not keep the Duchess waiting, and she hurried back down the long passage to the Drawing-Room.

The sun coming through the windows made her think that like Jeanie she would far sooner be in the garden than having what she was certain would be an uncomfortable interview with the Duchess.

She shut the door behind her and walked towards the fireplace.

As she expected, the Duchess was sitting in her usual chair on the right-hand side of the mantelpiece.

She was looking even more disagreeable than usual and, Pepita thought, although she knew it was uncharitable, exceedingly plain.

When she reached the Duchess she curtseyed and decided it would be correct not to sit down until she was asked to do so.

There was a perceptible pause before the Duchess said:

"I want to talk to you, Miss Linford."

Pepita did not reply, and again there was a pause before the Duchess said almost grudgingly:

"You can sit!"

"Thank you," Pepita replied quietly.

She chose the chair nearest to where the Duchess was sitting. It had a straight back and she sat upright in it with her hands clasped together in her lap.

She could feel very clearly the vibrations of hatred coming towards her from the Duchess, and she wondered if anybody else could have been able to feel them in the same way.

But perhaps in fact she had what her father called an "intuition" about people that was exceptional.

At last, after what seemed a long pause, the Duchess said:

"I am sure you have realised by this time, Miss Linford, that your presence here, as well as that of the two children you brought to the Castle uninvited, is causing me a great deal of distress."

It was not what Pepita had expected her to say and she answered quickly:

"I am deeply sorry, Your Grace, that we should upset you, especially at this particular time. But as I have already explained, there was nowhere else I could go, and I felt it must be right for them to be in the home of their ancestors."

"That is a matter of opinion!" the Duchess argued sharply. "So I have a suggestion to make which I think would solve both your problem and mine."

There was another pause before Pepita said, as if it was up to her to be encouraging:

"I. . .I am listening."

"I realise from what you have said," the Duchess went on, "that you have no money and the children were left penniless, which does not surprise me! I have been thinking what can be done about it."

Pepita was just about to say that it did not matter so much now that their grandfather was looking after them, went the Duchess went on:

"I am therefore offering you a thousand pounds, Miss Linford, if you will take the children away so that they disappear as their father did, out of sight and reach of my husband and myself."

Pepita was so surprised that she could only stare at the Duchess as if she could not believe what she had just heard.

"One thousand pounds is a lot of money," the Duchess went on, "and you will find, I am certain, that it is very advantageous from your own point of view. I will also contrive that five hundred pounds is paid every year into any Bank you nominate so long as you keep this arrangement completely secret from my husband and all other members of the McNairn family."

She spoke slowly and decisively, as if she had thought out every word before she spoke it.

Only when she had finished and Pepita realised she was waiting for her answer did she manage to say:

"I find it. . .incredible that Your Grace should think such an. . .extraordinary plan possible. . .even if I agreed to. . .accept the money you are offering me."

"It is perfectly possible!" the Duchess replied sharply. "I will arrange for a ship to take you away at night, and I have been thinking that you could either go back to England, where you came from, or if you prefer to the Shetland Islands, where it is very unlikely that anybody would find you."

"And you think that would be a proper place in which the future Duke of Strathnairn should be brought up?" Pepita asked.

Now she could feel her anger rising, and her first sense of shock at what the Duchess had suggested was giving way to indignation that anything so outrageous as far as the children were concerned had even entered her mind.

"The Duke exiled his son Alistair for his disloyalty and almost treacherous behaviour in marrying an English-woman, and without his permission," the Duchess retorted.

She paused, then as Pepita did not speak she went on:

"When he died he was no longer a member of the Clan, but an outcast, an exile! His children must pay for his sins and accept the same position that he had in his lifetime."

"You may think that, Your Grace," Pepita replied, "but now that the Duke has seen how much Rory resembles his father and himself, and that he is a true McNairn, I do not believe even for a moment that the boy could disappear without the Duke making a thorough search for him."

"My husband will do what I want," the Duchess said sharply, "and I am determined that if I have a son he shall be the next Duke of Strathnairn!"

Her voice rang out with an unmistakable note of defiance in it, and Pepita knew this was the whole crux of the problem.

"I can understand Your Grace's feelings," she said quietly. "At the same time, I could never in any circum-stances agree to deprive my nephew of his birthright."

She drew a deep breath before she went on:

"What is more, as my sister would have done if she were still alive, I will fight for his right to take the place to which he is entitled by birth."

Now her voice was almost as defiant as the Duchess's.

For a moment the two women stared at each other, and Pepita had the strange feeling that if they had been men they might now be fighting physically.

But she knew she was indeed fighting with every instinct and every nerve in her body, and her intuition told her that the Duchess was a formidable enemy who would try by every means in her power to get what she wanted.

There seemed no point in any further words, and they strove in silence each to impose her will on the other until the Duchess said, and her voice seemed almost to rasp in the silence of the room:

"Very well, Miss Linford, but I think you are very stupid and very obstinate, and whatever happens in the future will be entirely your fault!"

"I can only hope, Your Grace," Pepita replied, "that for Rory's sake you will remember that he is only a child, and children are very vulnerable to what older people feel about them."

"That is quite enough, Miss Linford!" the Duchess snapped. "As you have refused my offer, I can only hope that you have enough money of your own to support yourself when you leave here."

Her voice was slow and spiteful as she went on:

"His Grace has already decided that Rory should have a Tutor, and I am at the moment looking for a Scottish Governess to take care of them both so that your services will no longer be required!"

As she spoke the Duchess rose from her chair and, walking slowly but with a certain amount of dignity, left the room.

For a moment Pepita was unable to move and was finding it hard to think.

It seemed incredible that the Duchess should really have tried to bribe her to take the children away.

She knew she had been right in thinking that every day her dislike of them had increased to the point where she was prepared to do anything to get them out of her sight.

Pepita could imagine only too clearly what their life

would be in the Shetland Islands, which were bleak and practically uninhabited.

Even in England things would be little better: she had no home to go to and would be faced with the responsibility of planning the children's whole future herself.

"She is mad to think that such an idea would ever work!" Pepita cried. "Even if we did disappear, I am sure the Duke would search for Rory at any rate."

And yet she could not be sure of anything.

After all, it still seemed completely and utterly incredible that the Duke could have wiped his son Alistair out of his life as if he had never existed.

He had never, as far as she knew, made the slightest effort to find out if Alistair was alive or dead from the moment he had married her sister.

"How can they all be so insensitive and so cruel?" she asked herself.

At the same time she was really very frightened. For although she told herself she was being ridiculous, she could not help being apprehensive of what the Duchess might do.

She could hardly bear to allow herself to imagine that the Duchess might try to hurt Rory in some way, and yet her anxiety told her it was a possibility, and something she should not ignore.

"What shall I do?" she asked herself, as she had done last night.

She knew the problem was too big for her to solve alone and she must talk to Torquil.

She had told herself that after what had happened on the Watch-Tower, she must not risk revealing her love for him to other people, and therefore she must avoid him.

Yet now she knew she needed his help, his understanding, and, above everything else, his closeness to give her strength.

"I must find a way of talking to him," she decided as

she walked slowly back down the corridor towards the Housekeeper's room.

Jeanie, as she had expected, was so excited by the new-born kittens that she was only reluctantly dragged away from them to go out into the garden.

There she ran after butterflies, looked for fairies amongst the flowers, and spent a long time watching the goldfish swimming amongst the water-lilies in the fountain.

The fact that Jeanie was fully occupied with such interests left Pepita free to think, but she felt that everything was jumbled chaotically in her mind.

She knew too that she could make no decision without first speaking to Torquil.

Even to think of him made her love seem to sweep through her body like a tidal-wave.

She wanted him so urgently that she felt as if she sent her thoughts to him on wings and he must be aware of them.

'They always say the Scots are fey,' she thought, 'so if he loves me he should be aware that I need him and that only he can help me.'

The afternoon seemed to pass very slowly, and only when the Duchess, Pepita, and Jeanie were already seated at the tea-table did the guns return.

Rory came rushing into the room, not in the least tired after what the older men said had been quite a strenuous walk on the moors.

Full of excitement, he flung his arms round Pepita.

"Tomorrow I am going shooting with Hector and the Keeper, Aunt Pepita," he cried. "Grandpapa said he has a gun for me, and he will have the first bird I shoot stuffed so that I can keep it for ever and ever!"

He was so thrilled that his words seemed to fall over one another, and Pepita, holding him close, felt that the Duke would not part with him easily.

At the same time, as she looked at him at the end of

93

the table, stern, determined, and, she thought, ruthless, she could not be sure.

Torquil arrived after all the other guests were already seated, and as he entered the room Pepita felt her heart miss a beat.

Despite her resolution not to look at him with other people present, she could not prevent her eyes from seeking his.

As he entered he was looking at her as if he too could not help himself. Then when he saw the expression on her face he walked towards her and sat down in the empty chair that was next to Jeanie's.

"What have you been doing this afternoon?" he asked in a pleasant, conversational tone.

"We have been in the garden," Pepita replied.

Her eyes told him a different story, and she knew, almost as if he had spoken the words aloud, that he was aware she was worried and upset and wanted to tell him about it.

Then, as if he remembered he must be careful, he said to Jeanie:

"Did you catch a butterfly?"

"I tried and tried," Jeanie replied, "but it was easier to catch the little goldfish in the fountain. I held one in my hand before it slipped away."

"You must show me how you do it," he said.

"It is difficult, but I will show you," Jeanie promised.

"We will do that after tea," Torquil replied.

Pepita gave a sigh.

No-one else, she thought, could have been quick enough to understand and so clever in finding a way in which they could talk to each other.

"You must finish your tea first," she said to Jeanie, "and I expect everyone is hungry after walking such a long way high up on the moors."

"We walked for miles," Rory said, "and Grandpapa said I was very good and kept in line."

"That is true," one of the other guests agreed, "he is a real McNairn. They can always out-walk and out-shoot ordinary mortals like myself! I admit to being very foot-weary."

There followed an animated discussion about how far they had walked, but Pepita was waiting eagerly for tea to end, knowing that Jeanie would not forget Torquil's promise to watch her catch a goldfish.

It seemed a long time before the Duke, who had eaten very little, rose from his place at the table, and when he went from the room the Duchess followed him.

Jeanie got down from her chair and went to Torquil's side.

"Are you coming with me, Uncle Torquil?" she asked.

It was Torquil who had suggested she should call him "Uncle Torquil."

"There are far too many cousins about the place," he had said to Pepita, "and the child will get muddled with them. Moreover, if I had a niece I would want her to be exactly like Jeanie!"

"I think you are too young to be her uncle," Pepita had remarked.

"I want him to be my uncle!" Jeanie had said positively, " 'cause, although you are my aunt, I have never had an uncle before!"

"Then that is decided," Torquil had said, picking the small girl up in his arms. "I am your Uncle Torquil, and you are my adorable niece. When you are old enough I shall give a Ball for you in my Castle, and you will dance the Reels with the most handsome gentlemen in Scotland, all wearing their kilts."

Jeanie had been entranced by this idea and had talked about it until she went to bed.

"How long will I have to wait until I have my Ball,

Aunt Pepita?" she had enquired as Pepita tucked her up.

"Quite a number of years, I am afraid," Pepita had answered, "and first you will have to learn how to dance the Reels. We must find out if there is somebody in the Castle who can teach you."

"I would like that," Jeanie had said sleepily, "and Rory must learn them too."

Pepita had not forgotten, but there had been no opportunity to ask the Duke who could teach the children the Reels, and she knew it was not a suggestion which would find favour with the Duchess.

Now as she followed Jeanie, who was holding Torquil's hand, down the stairs to the Hall, she wondered where they all would be by the time Jeanie was grown up.

She had the frightening feeling that it would certainly not be here in the Castle, since, however impossible it might seem, the Duchess would somehow contrive to get rid of them.

The sun was sinking and the shadows were lengthening in the garden.

The wind, which had been high in the morning, had dropped. Now everything seemed quiet and beautiful and there was an atmosphere of peace and security about the great Castle rising above them and the unruffled surface of the sea.

But for Pepita there was a feeling of being menaced, a fear of danger from which she could not escape.

Jeanie was chattering away about the fish, and as she put her small hands into the water amongst the green leaves, Torquil was watching her.

Then suddenly she jumped up to run to the other side of the fountain.

"There are more fish here, Uncle Torquil!" she cried.

He moved closer to Pepita.

"What has upset you?" he asked quietly.

"You knew I was upset?"

"I knew it when I was coming back from the moor," he said. "I felt you needed me."

"I need you. . .desperately!"

"I was sure of it!"

She looked into his eyes and felt as if she surrendered herself into his arms and there would be no more problems, no more difficulties.

He was there, he loved her, and nothing else could matter.

Then she told herself that she had to think not only of herself but of the children.

"It is the. . .Duchess," she said in a low voice.

"I guessed that," Torquil replied. "What has she done now?"

"I cannot tell you here," Pepita said quickly, "but I must talk to you somehow."

As she spoke she realised that they were within sight of the Castle windows, and if the Duchess saw them together she might be more unpleasant than she had been the very first day when she had accused them of flirting with each other.

As if he understood without words, Torquil walked round to the opposite side of the fountain and took Jeanie by the hand.

"I have something to show you in the woods," he said. "We will catch a fish another day. I expect they are frightened now because you have caught one already."

"What are you going to show me in the woods?" Jeanie asked, instantly diverted.

"A little house in the trees that I had made for me many years ago, when I was about the same age as Rory," Torquil answered. "It may have become unsafe and dilapidated by now, but if you like it, I will have it repaired so that you can play in it."

Jeanie was obviously thrilled at this idea, and Torquil

led them out of the formal garden and into the woods which surrounded one side of the Castle and protected it from the winds which in the winter were often tempestuous.

As soon as they were out of sight of the Castle, Torquil said to Jeanie:

"Run along this path to see if you can find my house in the trees before I show you where it is. You will have to look carefully because it is well hidden."

Obediently Jeanie did as he said, and as soon as she was out of ear-shot Torquil said:

"My darling, you look so worried, and I want you to be happy."

"How can I be happy when such. . .strange things are. . .happening?" Pepita asked.

"Tell me about them," Torquil said.

Because it was so wonderful to have him there and to know that he would listen to her, Pepita could not prevent herself from slipping her hand into his.

His fingers closed over hers and she felt a thrill run through her in the same way as it had done the night when he had kissed her in the moonlight.

While she was thinking of his kisses, as if he read her thoughts, his eyes were on her lips as he said:

"It is an agony not to be able to kiss you and to tell you how beautiful you look and how much I want you."

He was speaking with a deep note in his voice which made it hard for her to breathe, and with an effort Pepita said:

"Please. . .I have to. . .tell you what has. . .happened."

"Tell me," he said, "and do not be afraid. I am here, and nothing shall harm you."

Yet, when she told him what the Duchess had said, he was aware that she was in fact very frightened.

"There is nothing that woman can do," he said when she had finished. "I am quite certain, whatever she may say, that if the children should disappear the Duke would make every effort to find them and bring them back."

"You really think that?" Pepita asked.

"I was watching him with Rory when we were on the moors," Torquil answered, "and there is no doubt that he is delighted with the boy and proud of him."

"That is what I want to hear."

"At the same time, I admit he is unpredictable, and the way in which he treated Alistair is incredible. But he had two sons in those days."

"He may have another son now," Pepita answered in a low voice, "and then Rory may no longer. . .interest him."

"I think he has mellowed with age," Torquil said, "and I am quite certain, although he would die rather than admit it, that after Euan was killed he wanted Alistair back with him, but was too stiff-necked and proud to try to find him."

"But now he has. . .Rory."

"As you say, now he has Rory," Torquil agreed, "and I do not believe he would give him up easily or, because he is a stickler for tradition, allow him to be supplanted by any son the Duchess may produce."

"There is not only the question of Rory's rightful place," Pepita said, "but the harm it could do to the children to be brought up in an atmosphere poisoned by the Duchess's obvious hatred of them."

She drew in her breath before she went on:

"I have only to see the way she looks at them, apart from the way she speaks to them, to be aware that she is exuding hatred like some evil witch. She would murder them if she would dare to do so!"

Torquil laughed.

"Darling, you are letting your imagination run away with you! Although I admit the Duchess is exceedingly rude and is making herself particularly unpleasant, I do not believe even a McDonavan would stoop to murder!"

"You cannot be. . .sure," Pepita murmured.

"I can only promise that I will not only look after you, which I intend to do, but also the children. No harm shall come to them while I am here."

"And if you. . .are not?"

"We will cross that bridge when we come to it," Torquil said. "At the moment, as you know, the Duke relies on me to run things for him and behaves as if I were his heir. But now that Rory is here, I am only too willing to act as Regent on his behalf."

"With no. . .regrets?"

"Not in the slightest!" he answered. "I am not ambitious in that sort of way. I have no wish to be Chieftain of the Clan, with all its problems and difficulties and endless complaints from those who have nobody else to complain to."

Pepita laughed.

"Then what are your ambitions?"

She spoke lightly, but Torquil's voice when he answered her was low and serious.

"To be married to you, my darling," he said, "so that we can live in peace and quiet with our children, and be happy ever after!"

What he said and the way his eyes rested on hers made Pepita feel as if she were in his arms and he was kissing her. It was impossible to think as she felt thrills rippling through her like waves of the sea.

Then, as she told herself it was something that would never happen, she heard Jeanie calling them.

"I have found it! I have found it!" she cried. "Oh, Uncle Torquil, please, can I climb up into it?"

It was a little wooden house with a thatched roof which could be reached by any agile child and was, Pepita thought, a perfect place for them to play.

After Torquil had climbed up into it himself and found that despite the years it had stood empty, the floor, which had been made by one of the Estate carpenters, was strong enough to hold him, he lifted up first Jeanie, then Pepita.

It was constructed in a tree that stood almost on the edge of the woods and from it they had a magnificent view of the bay above which the Castle was situated, and the curve of the cliffs going north, which were much higher than those directly below them.

"What an attractive place," Pepita exclaimed, "and what fun it must have been for you to play here as a small boy!"

"I used to bring a friend here during the School holidays, and we would spend hours looking out to sea with a telescope and watching the pigeons coming home to the caves beneath the cliffs."

Pepita looked at him enquiringly, and he said:

"Did not Alistair tell you how the caves here are the nesting-places for thousands of pigeons? They do a great deal of damage to the crops, but it is fascinating to watch them going back to roost."

"I think I do remember his saying something about it," Pepita replied, "but I did not understand what happened."

"I must take young Rory to see them," Torquil said. "He would enjoy rowing into the caves in a boat to watch the pigeons come rushing out because one's voice echoes and re-echoes."

"I am sure Rory would love that," Pepita agreed.

As she spoke she thought what a good father Torquil would make for his own children when he had any.

Then, as if from the expression in her eyes he had read her thoughts, she felt the colour come into her cheeks.

There was no need for words.

They just looked at each other, and she knew they both were praying that by some miracle one day their dream of being together would come true.

It was now growing late, so they walked back to the Castle.

Only when Jeanie ran ahead to find Rory to tell him about the little house in the tree was Torquil able to say to Pepita:

"I love you, my darling, and if I cannot kiss you soon I shall go mad!"

"It is. . .impossible!"

"Nothing is impossible!" he declared. "Now that you know the way here, meet me after dinner."

"It is impossible!" Pepita said again quickly.

"There is still a moon," he went on as if she had not spoken, "and if you go to bed early, I will wait and leave at the same time as some of the other guests so that my absence will not be noticed."

"Supposing the Duchess. . .suspects that we are. . . meeting each other?" Pepita asked in a frightened voice.

"You can go out through the garden door," Torquil said. "None of the servants will see you leave the Castle. They all retire early, most of them having been here for years."

"Are you sure. . .quite sure it is. . .safe for us to do. . .this?"

"One can never be absolutely certain of anything," he answered, "and I have no wish, my precious one, for you to run any risks. At the same time, I must hold you in my arms and tell you how much I love you, otherwise I shall have another sleepless night!"

Pepita smiled, then she said teasingly:

"That obviously is. . .something that must be. . .prevented at all. . .costs!"

Torquil laughed, then he said seriously:

"I know I am being dramatic, but that is how you make me feel, and nobody, my darling, has ever made me feel like this before."

It was impossible to doubt his sincerity, and because

she wanted so much to see him, to be with him, to be kissed by him, she said:

"I feel it is something we. . .should not do. . .but if it is possible. . .I will. . .come to the woods."

"It will be possible tonight," Torquil said, "but soon the weather will change and we shall have to find somewhere inside the Castle where we can meet, which might prove far more dangerous."

She could understand the logic of what he was saying, but it was impossible to discuss it any further, for they had reached the door of the Castle and they could hear Jeanie calling for Rory as she ran up the main staircase.

* * *

It was, however, with a beating heart and a feeling that she was doing something wrong that Pepita left the Drawing-Room with Lady Rogart, who was the oldest guest present.

She had taken the precaution when she went into the Drawing-Room before dinner of carrying in her hand a silk shawl, as if she feared she might feel cold during the evening.

She had laid it on a chair just inside the door as she had seen other ladies do on previous evenings.

Picking it up now saved her from having to walk all the way back to her own bedroom on the West side of the Castle.

Lady Rogart's room was in the opposite direction, and as they said good-night, Pepita curtseyed and said:

"You are very pretty, my child, but I am afraid where women are concerned you will find it as much a handicap as an advantage."

Pepita had noticed the Duchess talking to Lady Rogart after dinner and had guessed some of the unpleasant things she must have said.

"Thank you for understanding," she replied. "At the same time, there is nothing I can do about it."

"And nothing you would want to do, if you were honest!" Lady Rogart said with a smile. "You will find that men will always be willing to help you and look after you, and it is only the women who will have very different ideas."

Because she spoke so kindly, Pepita had a sudden urge to tell Lady Rogart how difficult the Duchess was being.

Then she felt certain that Lady Rogart was already aware of it and there was nothing she could do.

'There is only one person to whom I can tell the truth and who will understand,' she thought.

As soon as Lady Rogart was out of sight she hurried downstairs to the garden door.

It was locked and bolted for the night, but she let herself out and closed the door behind her, hoping that when she returned she and Torquil would not find themselves locked out.

If they were, she was certain he would manage by some means of his own to get them back into the Castle again without anyone being aware of it.

"All I can do is to rely on him now and forever," she told herself. "Then there will be no more problems, I shall be safe, and so will the children."

She was not certain how she could be so sure that he would look after them, and she tried to tell herself that she only believed it possible because she was in love.

And yet she knew that her instinct was stronger than her mind, and though she had no sure grounds for thinking so, it would be Torquil who would keep them safe.

Outside it was once again a fairy-land of beauty with the stars twinkling in the sky, and the moon, although it was now on the wane, turning everything to silver.

It was easy to follow the small path twisting through

the trees where they had walked in the afternoon, and everything was very quiet.

The only sounds she could hear were those of small animals scurrying about in the undergrowth, and an occasional bird flew off in fright as she passed beneath the bough on which it had been roosting.

Because Pepita had always lived in the country she was not afraid of the darkness, and in Cornwall she had often gone for long walks after dinner so as to leave her sister and Alistair alone as they preferred to be.

Now she thought they must have felt, as she was feeling, pulsating with love and longing irrepressibly to be close to each other.

When she reached the tree with the little house she did not climb up to it, but leaned against the trunk and felt as if the peace and beauty of the stars and the moonlight moved into her heart.

Then as she waited, feeling almost as if the world were waiting with her, she saw a movement in the distance and knew that Torquil was coming towards her.

As he came a little nearer she could wait no longer but ran to him, wanting him so much that her whole body ached with an irresistible yearning for the strength of his arms.

He stood still until she reached him. Then he was holding her so tightly that it was impossible to breathe, and his lips were on hers.

He kissed her until the whole world swung dizzily round them. The stars seemed to fall down to cover them and a light came from both of them which was not human but Divine.

To Pepita it was as if she gave herself completely and utterly to the man whom she loved, and he took from her not only her heart but her soul.

She was a part of him as he was a part of her, and they were no longer two people but one.

Only when a century or longer seemed to have passed and they had touched the sky and were no longer on earth, did Pepita say in a voice that did not sound like her own:

"I. . .love. . .you. . .I. . .love you!"

"I worship you!" Torquil said. "How can I live without you? How can I exist unless you are with me and are my wife?"

He did not wait for her answer but was kissing her again until, as if the fierce, possessive demand of his lips was too intense to be borne, she made a little murmur and hid her face against his neck.

"My precious," he said, "I must not frighten you, but you do not know the agony it is to see you and not to touch you, and to know that you are sleeping beneath the same roof but I may not come near you."

There was a pain in the way he spoke, which told Pepita how much he suffered, and she said:

"We. . .must try to be. . .sensible."

"What is sensible?" he asked. "To know that the most priceless treasure any man could find or own is just out of reach? We cannot go on like this. I cannot bear it!"

"There is nothing. . .else we can do," Pepita answered. "I love you. . .but. . .I am afraid."

"I understood that when you talked about it before," Torquil said, "but I have had an idea, and I want to discuss it with you."

"What. . .is it?" Pepita asked apprehensively.

"We must first find somewhere where we can sit," he said. "I will not take you up into the house in the tree in case you hurt yourself."

Instead he led her off the path to where there was a little clearing where some trees had fallen in a gale.

It was bright in the moonlight, and Torquil drew Pepita to where there was a fallen trunk on which they both could sit.

He put his arms round her and drew her close against him as he said:

"Now listen to me, my darling. I have been thinking, after you told me what the Duchess had said to you, that it might be a good idea for me to speak to the Duke."

"About what?" Pepita asked in a frightened tone.

"I will tell him that I love you and want to marry you, and that when we are married we will take the children, since they are upsetting the Duchess, with us to my own Castle."

Just for a moment Pepita thought that it would be the most perfect thing she could think of to be married to Torquil and not to be afraid for Rory and Jeanie.

Then she gave a little cry of protest.

"No. . .no!" she said. "You cannot do that!"

"Why not?"

"First of all, the Duke has already. . .decided to get rid of. . .me."

"What do you mean by that?"

"I forgot to tell you that the Duchess said she had persuaded him to have a Tutor for Rory and a Scottish Governess for Jeanie."

"Are you sure she said that?" Torquil enquired.

"Yes, but I was so perturbed by her suggestion that I should take them away secretly that I really forgot about it until now."

There was silence. Then Torquil said:

"It certainly sounds, if that is what the Duke intends, that the children are to be looked after without you."

"I realise that now," Pepita said. "But, Torquil, I cannot leave them without being afraid. . .but I am not. . .certain what I can. . .do."

"You can marry me!"

She shook her head, but he said:

"I will marry you whether you agree or not. How can

107

you possibly be alone in the world with nobody to look after you?"

"I would have to. . .find some. . .work to do," Pepita said a little helplessly.

"It is not a question of work," Torquil said. "You are far too lovely to be alone. There are men who would pursue you, and how do you think I would feel, knowing you were struggling on your own?"

He spoke fiercely, and as if the idea upset him he pulled her roughly against him and kissed her again.

Now his lips were passionate and demanding. She knew that he was subduing her with his kisses, showing his domination and making her realise she was his.

It did not frighten her, instead she felt something wild and wonderful leap within her towards the fire on his lips and the love which was beating in his breast.

She felt it flowing from him, seeping through her, and as she responded to it and he held her closer and still closer, she felt as if he took possession of her.

There was no longer any need for her to think or to be worried or to try to decide anything.

She was his, completely and absolutely, to do with as he would.

Then the sound of an owl hooting in the woods brought them back to sanity.

With their hearts beating wildly, their eyes seeming to glint with a burning light, they looked at each other for a long moment.

"You are mine!" Torquil said fiercely. "Mine, and nothing in the whole world will stop me from loving you and keeping you with me from now throughout eternity!"

"I. . .love. . .you!" Pepita whispered.

He would have kissed her again but she put up her hands.

"Please, darling please. . .do not make me love you

any more. It. . .frightens me, not because I am afraid. . .but because it is so. . .perfect. . .so wonderful!"

As if he understood, he took her hands in his and raised them one after the other to his lips.

As he did so, Pepita realised she was trembling with the intensity of her feelings and that he was too.

"I adore you," he said, "and because I am trying to think of you rather than of myself, I will take you back, but somehow I am going to find a solution to this damned mess, as quickly as possible!"

The determination in the way he spoke was inescapable and she knew, although it seemed impossible, that because he was who he was and because love was greater than anything else, he would find a way.

Reluctantly, and because it was difficult to move after the rapture he had given her, Pepita rose to her feet.

Torquil rose too and for a moment she just looked at him, thinking how handsome he was in his kilt and velvet jacket with a lace jabot at his throat.

The moonlight was full on both of them and she felt as if his head were encircled with stars and they gave him a power against which no human difficulties could prevail.

Then very gently, in a very different way from the tempest through which they had just passed, Torquil drew her close to him again.

He kissed her lips, but now there was no fire, only a tenderness that made the tears come into Pepita's eyes.

"Believe in me and trust me," he said, "and with the help of God, you and I will win."

He put her hand through his arm and they walked slowly and in silence back along the path through the woods towards the Castle.

Chapter Six

The next day was Sunday, and as Pepita was getting Jeanie ready for the Kirk, Rory came rushing into the room to show her that he was wearing the kilt for the first time.

Mrs. Sutherland had told Pepita that she was unearthing the clothes that Alistair and his brother had worn when they were children, and she was sure there would be a complete outfit for Rory, including a sporran and a small skean-dhu.

Now dressed in his finery, Rory was delighted with himself.

"Now I look like a real Scot!" he exclaimed proudly. "Any Sassenach who gets in my way I shall fight with my skean-dhu!"

"I am a Sassenach," Pepita said quietly.

"Oh, I do not mean you, Aunt Pepita," Rory said. "I love you, and whatever you were, you would still be my favourite aunt."

Pepita laughed.

"That is a very big compliment, considering I am the only aunt you have!"

But Rory was not listening. He was looking at himself in the mirror and admiring his sporran, which he knew was a small replica of the one his grandfather wore in the daytime.

"I want to have a kilt too," Jeanie said plaintively.

"If we can buy some tartan I will make you one," Pepita promised, "but you look very pretty as you are."

It was true. In her pink coat and bonnet trimmed with tiny roses she looked like a small flower.

It seemed impossible that even somebody as hard-hearted as the Duchess could dislike her.

They drove to the Kirk, which was not far from the Castle, in three carriages, and while Rory travelled with his grandfather and the Duchess, Pepita and Jeanie were with Lady Rogart and her husband.

Torquil was with three other guests in the last carriage, and when they reached the Kirk, Pepita found that she and Jeanie were in the second pew behind the Duke and Duchess and Rory and Torquil.

As she knelt and prayed, it was difficult not to be acutely aware of the man just in front of her, and during the Service she found that her eyes kept straying to his broad shoulders and the way his hair was cut so neatly at the back of his neck.

Even to be near him made her feel as if her love welled up inside her, so that as well as her prayers her whole being was filled with an awareness of him.

The Kirk was very austere and the Minister did not wear a surplice but only a black cassock.

He was a gaunt, ageing man with hard features, and when he climbed into the pulpit Pepita expected to hear a sermon denouncing sinners and threatening them with dire punishments in the next world.

Instead his sermon was a long discourse on the iniquities which the English had perpetrated on the Scots.

She realised he was speaking of what had happened when the Scottish were defeated at the battle of Cullodon and how they had suffered in the ensuing years.

Not only were their lands and their arms taken from them but also their tartans and their kilts.

They had suffered cruelly, she thought; no-one could dispute that.

At the same time the Minister spoke as if it had happened yesterday, and she found it hard to realise that it was all quite ancient history and there was nobody left alive who could remember what had occurred.

Then as the Minister went on and on, inciting, she thought, the feelings of those who listened against the English, she knew despairingly that it would be impossible for her ever to marry Torquil, whatever he might say.

How could she live in an atmosphere where she was not only despised and hated but, because she was English, was considered responsible for the atrocities that had taken place more than a hundred years before she was born?

What was more, how could she ever bring her children to Church for them to hear perhaps Sunday after Sunday such a discourse, knowing that every word accused their mother of belonging to what to them was a criminal race?

"It is hopeless," she told herself despairingly, and once again she knew she must go away.

What at last the sermon ended and she knelt to pray, Pepita had the greatest difficulty in controlling her tears and preventing them from running down her cheeks.

They drove back in the same order as they had come, and Pepita wondered as she sat in the carriage if Torquil was feeling, as she did, that any union between them was impossible.

Because the attack was so bitter and made her so miserable, she wanted to cry out at the injustice of it.

But by the time she had tidied Jeanie and Rory and washed their hands before luncheon, she had control of herself.

When she took the children to the Drawing-Room she held her head high and there was a look of defiance in her eyes. She would not humble herself to the Scots, whatever they might feel about her.

Nevertheless, as they sat at the great Dining-Room table with the Duke at its head, looking every inch a Chieftain, she knew she could expect no mercy from a race who never forget.

* * *

The last members of the house-party were to leave after luncheon, and as they talked of their journeys to other parts of Scotland, Torquil said to Rory:

"You and I are going on a journey later today."

"Where to?" Rory asked.

"I am going to take you to see the pigeon caves."

"I have heard about them from Grandpapa," Rory replied excitedly. "Shall we take a gun to frighten the birds out of the caves?"

"As it is Sunday we will have to make do with our voices," Torquil replied. "I assure you that if we shout very loudly, they will come flying out and disappear so quickly over the edge of the cliff that you will find it impossible to count them."

"I shall try!" Rory exclaimed.

"You must be careful, Torquil!" the Duke said. "Remember that if the boat is dashed against the rocks and overturned, not even the strongest swimmer has a chance in the currents at this point."

"I have not forgotten," Torquil replied with a smile.

"I have been there so often that I assure you I know every rock and every place that is dangerous for at least five miles along the coast."

Rory was so excited at going to see the caves that he found it difficult to settle and do anything else for the rest of the afternoon.

Torquil arranged that they should have an early tea, and because it seemed the sensible thing to do, Pepita and Jeanie joined them at the tea-table just before four o'clock.

"I want to go in the boat!" Jeanie said as soon as she realised what her brother was doing.

"I will take you another day," Torquil promised.

"I want to go with you now, Uncle Torquil!" Jeanie persisted.

"I tell you what we will do," Pepita interposed, knowing that Jeanie felt she was being deprived of a special treat. "We will go to the little house in the trees and watch them from there."

The child cheered up immediately, and as soon as tea was finished Torquil and Rory went through the garden and down to the Quay where the boats belonging to the Castle were moored.

Pepita and Jeanie set off in the opposite direction through the woods, but when they reached the little house Pepita realised that there were so many leaves on the trees that it might be difficult to see the boat if it kept close to the cliffs.

"What we will have to do is to walk along the edge of the cliffs," she said to Jeanie, "and wave to Rory and Uncle Torquil as they pass us. Then afterwards we will climb up to the little house."

Jeanie was quite amenable to this suggestion, and they wandered through the trees onto the rough ground which lay between the woods and the sea.

As they arrived there they saw that they had taken longer to get there than Pepita had anticipated, and already the boat containing Torquil and Rory was almost ahead of them.

"We must run," Jeanie said, "or they will not see us!"

She started to run quickly over the rough ground, and as she did so Pepita saw about twenty yards ahead of them on the edge of the cliff something which looked, she thought, like a large animal lying down.

Jeanie was running towards it, and it flashed through Pepita's mind that it could be one of the cattle, which might get up and frighten her.

Then as she hurried after the child she saw that it was not an animal but a person.

Somebody was lying on the very edge of the cliff, and it occurred to her that it was a very strange thing to do.

Then as Jeanie, intent on looking at the boat which contained her brother, had almost reached the person lying down, Pepita saw that it was a woman, and although it seemed incredible, it was the Duchess.

There was no mistaking, now that she was nearer, the fawn-coloured tweed that Her Grace had been wearing at luncheon, which blended with the rough grass so that it appeared almost as if she were camouflaged.

It flashed through Pepita's mind that the Duchess must have fallen down by accident or because she felt ill.

Then incredibly she saw that in her hands she was holding a rifle.

It seemed strange that she should be practising shooting at the sea, until with a sense of shock Pepita realised as she drew nearer still that the Duchess was training her sights on the boat which was being rowed by Torquil and was almost opposite her.

In the flash of a second, although it seemed very much longer, Pepita understood what the Duchess was intending to do.

The warning the Duke had given Torquil at luncheon, that the sea at this particular point was so dangerous that the strongest swimmer would not survive in it, came to her mind as if written in letters of fire.

She knew that if the Duchess's aim was successful, the boat would sink and both Rory and Torquil would be drowned.

She rushed forward, but Jeanie had reached the Duchess before her.

"Is that a gun?" she heard the child ask.

The Duchess, intent òn what she was doing, had not heard Jeanie approach, but now she turned her head and there was an expression of fury on her face.

"What are you doing here?" she demanded. "Go away and leave me alone!"

The angry way in which she spoke astonished Jeanie. Then, as if she was aware of what the Duchess was doing, she said:

"It is wrong to shoot on Sundays!"

The Duchess made an inarticulate sound of rage.

Then, realising that Pepita was just behind Jeanie, she said furiously:

"Get out of my way, both of you, and mind your own business!"

As she spoke she rose from the prone position in which she had been lying, and seemed to point her rifle at Jeanie. Frightened, Jeanie took a step back from her, and in doing so she stumbled on the edge of the cliff.

She gave a shout of fear, and only by flinging herself forward on the ground did Pepita manage to catch hold of her arm as she fell.

But Jeanie's weight was too much to enable her to pull the child to safety, and she hung over the edge with Pepita holding her by the wrist and with her other hand catching hold of her coat.

Jeanie was screaming in fear, and for the moment, with the force of her fall, Pepita had the breath knocked out of her body.

Then she realised that the Duchess had risen to her knees, and now as if what had happened made her completely lose control of herself, she screamed:

"Let her fall—and the boy shall die too! He shall not—stop my son from—inheriting!"

As she spoke she raised the rifle to her shoulder, trying to aim it on the boat beneath her.

It was then that Pepita found her voice.

"Stop! Stop!" she shouted. "You cannot commit. . . murder! It is wicked!"

"He shall die! Both of them shall die!" the Duchess retorted furiously.

From the hysterical way in which she spoke, Pepita now knew that she was mad.

She was still struggling frantically to pull Jeanie back over the edge of the cliff, but while the child screamed and trembled, she had not the strength to do it, though she tried to lever herself backwards.

Even as she struggled she was aware that the Duchess was intending to kill Rory and Torquil, and somehow she found enough breath to cry out:

"Help. . .Oh, God!. . .Help them!"

Then, when she expected any moment to hear the report of the rifle and know that the Duchess had been successful, a deep voice said behind them:

"Stop, Yer Grace, an' gi' me the rifle!"

Once again, just as she was about to pull the trigger the Duchess turned her head.

"Go away!" she snarled. "They have to die—and no-one shall—stop me!"

It was then that Pepita was aware that Hector, the Head Keeper who had taken Rory out fishing, was reaching out to take the rifle from the Duchess's hands.

"Leave me alone!" she shouted. "How dare you interfere! I will have you dismissed for your impertinence!"

"Even so Oi'll take th' gun," Hector replied sharply.

There was a struggle as the Keeper tried to take the gun from the Duchess's hands, but she was fighting with him, struggling to her feet and at the same time pulling at the rifle, determined that he should not have it.

Then as Jeanie's screams added to the confusion, Hector managed to wrench the rifle from the Duchess, and as she frantically resisted, she slipped on the grass and fell.

There was just one ear-splitting scream as she disappeared over the edge.

The horror of what had happened seemed to envelop Pepita like a dark cloud, and at the same time she felt Hector pull Jeanie to safety.

Then, for the first time in her life, she fainted.

She must have been unconscious for some time, because she came back through the dark to hear Jeanie crying:

"Wake up, Aunt Pepita, wake up! I's frightened!"

With an effort Pepita managed to sit up, and now she saw that she and Jeanie were alone and she guessed that Hector had gone to fetch help.

Because she knew it was the right thing to do, she tried to breathe deeply.

She was very cold, which she knew came from fear, and it was difficult to think clearly and even her eyes seemed to be out of focus.

She managed, however, to put her arms closer round the child and held her against her.

"I fell over the cliff!" Jeanie was saying tearfully. "If you had not held on to me I would have fallen into the sea!"

"But. . .you are. . .safe."

Then as Pepita spoke she wondered if Rory and Torquil were safe too.

It was difficult, now that it was over, to remember exactly what had happened.

She had a sudden fear that the Duchess had fired at the boat before Hector had arrived to take the rifle from her.

Then she was sure that she had not had time to do so.

The Duchess had fallen, and somehow she must get Jeanie back to the Castle before the child was aware of the tragedy that had taken place.

"I fell over the cliff," Jeanie replied. "I's frightened, very, very frightened!"

"You are. . .quite safe now," Pepita said again weakly.

She knew she must get on her feet and walk back to the Castle, but she found it impossible to move.

Then as she put her hand up to her forehead to find it wet with sweat even though she was cold, she saw in the distance a man running towards them.

Because her heart gave a leap even before she was able to identify him, she knew instinctively who it was.

As if Jeanie was aware that the one person who could help them was Torquil, she moved from Pepita's arms, saying:

"There is Uncle Torquil. I shall go and tell him how frightened I was."

She ran towards him as she spoke, and once again Pepita told herself she must get to her feet.

But she could do no more than watch Torquil as he picked Jeanie up in his arms and kissed her.

Then, carrying the child, he moved more slowly towards her, and she knew that God had saved him and Rory from being murdered.

*　　*　　*

Lying comfortably in bed, with Mrs. Sutherland fussing over her, Pepita knew that everything was different from the moment Torquil had reached her.

She had not only ceased to struggle against her

weakness, but because he was there the horror of what had happened seemed to recede and gradually she was able to breathe normally.

He had knelt down beside her and taken her hand in his and kissed it before he said:

"I saw everything that happened, my darling, and you saved not only Jeanie's life but also mine and Rory's."

"It was. . .Hector who did. . .that," Pepita murmured.

She realised that Torquil was not listening.

"I want you to go back to the Castle while I try to arrange about the Duchess."

"She is. . .dead?"

"Yes, she is dead," Torquil confirmed quietly.

He drew Pepita to her feet and carried her back through the woods until she said she could walk on her own.

Jeanie had run ahead of them to find Rory, whom Torquil had sent straight back to the Castle.

He had given him instructions to tell Fergus, the footmen, and anybody else who was available, to go to the top of the cliffs, and also to take a boat round to where the Duchess had fallen.

Only when he was alone with Pepita did he say in a voice that told her how deeply he was upset by what had occurred:

"My precious darling! You should not have been involved in anything so horrible!"

"She. . .she intended that Rory. . .should die!" Pepita whispered. "And. . .you might have. . .died too!"

"She was mad, though we did not realise it," Torquil replied. "But it is most important that, as far as the world is concerned, when she was walking along the cliffs she stumbled and fell."

He spoke sternly, as if he defied anybody to argue with him, and Pepita asked:

"Will you tell the Duke. . .the truth?"

Torquil nodded.

"He will know, and of course Hector, but nobody else, and the rifle will already be lost in the sea, so there will be no evidence to show what occurred."

Pepita shivered.

Although she was now walking, Torquil's arm was supporting her, and she had the feeling that nothing mattered because he was there.

"It is something you will have to forget, my darling," he said as they came in sight of the Castle, "and now I must leave you and go to find Hector and convince him that it was an accident."

"Yes. . .of course," Pepita agreed.

Only when she reached her own bedroom did she feel as if she might faint again.

Mrs. Sutherland undressed her as if she were a child, then slipped her nightgown over her head and helped her into bed.

"Where are the. . .children?" Pepita asked, feeling that she should be with them.

"Dinna fret, Miss, they're quite safe, an' I'll see to them while ye're restin'."

Pepita shut her eyes, thinking that all she wanted to do was to dream of Torquil holding her close against him and forget the horror of what had happened.

Even so, she thought it would be impossible ever to erase from her memory the agony she had felt in thinking that Rory and Torquil would drown and she would be unable to drag Jeanie back to safety.

It had all happened so quickly, but she felt as if the Duchess's mad voice and the scream she had given when she lost her balance and fell into the waves splashing high over the rocks below would remain in her memory forever.

"How could she have planned anything so. . .diabolical, so wicked?" she asked herself.

She knew that it was hatred that had eaten into her

like some terrible cancer which had gradually sent her mad.

'Hatred is as dangerous and lethal as any weapon,' Pepita thought, and found herself remembering once again that the Scots never forget.

Then as slowly her weakness passed and her mind cleared, she knew that now that the children were no longer menaced by the Duchess, as her instinct had told her they were from the very beginning, she must leave.

It was impossible to stay here loving Torquil and knowing that his love for her would destroy him as effectively as the Duchess would have done had she been successful in causing the boat in which he was rowing Rory to sink.

Now the Duke would need him even more than he had when Torquil had taken the place of the son he had banished.

It would be a very long time before Rory became old enough to be of any assistance.

'If I marry Torquil, it will destroy him!' Pepita thought.

Only to think of him made the tears, which she could no longer control, run down her cheeks, and she knew they came from her own weakness because her love consumed her whole body, and her heart was his.

But her mind and her determination told her that because she loved him she must do what was right for him, and the only way she could do that was to go away.

She knew it would be impossible to say good-bye or to have him plead with her today.

'I must disappear and go somewhere where he cannot find me,' she thought.

Then as she felt the pain of what this would mean flood into her as if a sword pierced her heart, she knew that the true love which she had for Torquil could not be selfish and self-centred.

However much she suffered, she must think of him first.

The mere thought of his handsome face, his arms round her, his lips seeking hers, made the tears run faster, and she felt as if each one of them might have been dipped in her blood.

'The sooner I go, the better,' she thought, 'because every day I linger will make it harder both for Torquil and for me.'

For a few days he would be very busy with the Duchess's Funeral, and he would have to help the Duke entertain not only the McNairns but also the McDonavans.

'That will be a good time to leave,' Pepita thought, 'when no-one will notice me.'

Once again she was up against the difficulty of having no money, in addition to having to decide where she should go and what she could do.

She felt that the most sensible thing would be to return to the small village where she and Denise had lived with their father until he died.

At least the people there knew her, and although there were few big houses, there were the Doctor and the Vicar and many of the tradespeople who knew her father well.

She felt sure they would help her until she could find work which at least would keep her alive.

'I shall have to ask somebody in the Castle to help me,' she thought and knew the only person in whom she could confide would be Mrs. Sutherland.

She was sure that she could swear her to secrecy and, although it seemed very reprehensible, persuade her to lend her just enough money for the train fare from Edinburgh to London.

Then she had another idea. She was not certain, but she imagined it might be cheaper to go by sea.

In which case there might be a fishing-boat that would

carry her from here to Edinburgh, and in Edinburgh she could transfer to a ship which would take her South.

It was the sort of thing she had never before had to plan on her own, but she told herself that now that she was alone, she had to be resolute and sensible enough to look after herself.

At the thought of the long years ahead without Torquil she found herself crying again and was ashamed that she should be so helpless.

It was quite late when Mrs. Sutherland came into the bedroom, carrying her dinner on a tray.

Because she was expecting her to return, Pepita had wiped her eyes and managed to sit up against her pillows, looking very pale but otherwise more or less normal.

"It's awfa' late we are, Miss. The whole place is that upset as ye can imagine, but I've brought ye a bite tae eat," Mrs. Sutherland said as she came into the room.

She put down the tray by the bedside and went on:

"They've found Her Grace drifting out to sea, but there was naught they could do to save her. Terrible bruises there were on her face from where she fell on the rocks!"

Pepita could not resist a little shudder as Mrs. Sutherland spoke, and the Housekeeper continued:

"Mr. Torquil is helping His Grace, and ye are not to worry aboot the bairns. They're both in their beds, tired out with all the excitement."

"I thought perhaps they would come to say goodnight to me," Pepita said.

"They wanted to, but I wouldna let them," Mrs. Sutherland replied. "Ye've had quite enough for one day! Ye're looking washed oot wi' it all! Now drink yer soup while it's hot an' it'll make ye feel better."

Pepita tried to do as she was told, but although a delicious dish of fish had been brought for her, it was impossible to eat more than a few mouthfuls.

She lay back, planning what she must do and longing for Torquil until she felt he must be aware of how desperately she needed him.

Only when Mrs. Sutherland came back to take away her tray and ask her if there was anything else she wanted for the night did she say in a rather frightened tone:

"I want your help, Mrs. Sutherland."

"Aye, o' course, Miss. What can I do fer ye?"

"I. . .I have to. . .go away," Pepita said, "and because I do not wish to. . .upset the children. . .or for them to have any idea that I am leaving them. . .I must go secretly. . .and no-one must be aware of it until I have. . . gone."

Mrs. Sutherland looked at her in surprise, then said:

"For what reason would ye be leaving when the children want ye? I'm thinking ye've bin happy here."

"Very. . .happy!" Pepita said with a little break in her voice. "At the same time, you must realise that because I am English, for me to go away is in the best interests of the children, who are Scottish."

"That is true," Mrs. Sutherland agreed. "At the same time, we've liked ye very much, Miss, and we felt when we got to know ye that we could understand why Lord Alistair married yer sister and found happiness outside his ain land."

"Thank you," Pepita said. "I shall always remember you said that, Mrs. Sutherland, but I know it is right for me to leave."

"Ye've somewhere tae go, Miss?"

It was impossible for Pepita to lie, and she gave a little sigh before she said:

"No, I must find somewhere. . .but it will be. . .very difficult as I have. . .no money."

She saw the surprise in Mrs. Sutherland's face, and she said quickly:

"If. . .perhaps you could lend me enough for my fare

South I promise I would repay you. . .but I do not wish to ask His Grace for it in case he inadvertently lets the children know that I am leaving them."

"They'll miss ye sorely," Mrs. Sutherland remarked.

"Children forget," Pepita replied briefly, "and there will be so many new and exciting things for them to do here that they will not miss me for long."

"I had heard," Mrs. Sutherland said tentatively, "that His Grace was intending tae find a Tutor for His wee Lordship."

"And it will not be. . .difficult to find a Governess for Lady Jeanie," Pepita added.

"That's true," Mrs. Sutherland agreed. "At the same time, she wouldna be their aunt, and as we always say: 'blood is thicker than water'!"

"I have to go!" Pepita said resolutely. "So please. . .help me. . .and promise me you will not say one word to anybody else in the Castle."

"I promise, if that's what ye ask me," Mrs. Sutherland said, "but how can ye get away wi'out anybody being aware of it?"

It was then that Pepita told Mrs. Sutherland her idea about a ship that would take her to Edinburgh.

"I'll make a few enquiries, Miss," Mrs. Sutherland said. "I've never moved very far frae the Castle masel', but others on the Estate have gone North and South, although I've never troubled to find out how they go aboot it."

Pepita gave a little laugh that had a hint of tears in it.

"This is a little world all its own, Mrs. Sutherland, and you are very lucky to belong to it."

She thought as she spoke that the only thing she longed for was to stay here with Torquil and live in his Castle and forget there was any world outside.

In the short time she had lived in Scotland she had learnt to understand how, with their sport and the closeness of the Clan clustering round their Chieftain, people had no need to envy the world outside.

There was so much to be done and so much satisfaction in doing it together with those who were blood-brothers and had the same interests and the same ambitions and drew the same comfort from a togetherness which she had not found in England.

She knew that if she were a Scot and a McNairn, she would be one of them and they would look after her.

Then it would be impossible to feel lonely or that the world was a great, frightening place in which she had nobody to turn to.

She remembered Rory saying, as Alistair had said, that the Chieftain was the father of his Clan, and that was what the Duke was to his people.

One day Rory would take his place, and he would belong to them as they belonged to him.

"The Scots are so lucky, so very, very lucky," Pepita told herself.

Then almost like the voice of doom she remembered that also they "never forget."

Although she was desperately tired, when Mrs. Sutherland left her she found it impossible to sleep.

She could only know that she had to leave, and everything she cared for, everything she loved, must be left behind.

To think of leaving Torquil was an agony that seemed to tear her apart, but she knew also how much it hurt her to leave Rory and Jeanie.

They were the only relatives she had left, and she felt that they were so much a part of herself that it would be like losing one of her limbs to part with them.

The light from the fire flickered in the great room in which she was sleeping, and she felt as though the shadows were full of ghosts from the past who were telling her of other men and women who had slept in this room and suffered as she had.

Yet they at least had belonged to the Castle and their Clan and had known that wherever they went in the world, there would always be somebody of their own kin to welcome them home and give them a helping hand.

"Could anybody be more lonely than I am?" Pepita asked in self-pity.

Then as she felt the tears come once again into her eyes so that the light from the fire seemed to swim dizzily in front of her, she heard the door open.

For a moment she thought it must be Jeanie coming in from the room next door.

Then she realised it was the door into the passage and gave a little gasp as she saw who was there.

Torquil shut the door behind him and came towards the bed.

"Why. . .are you. . .here. . .what do you. . .want?"

She spoke in a low voice, afraid that something terrible had happened.

"I had to see you, my darling," he answered. "I had the feeling you needed me, and I thought too, although I may be wrong, that you are unhappy."

Pepita gave a little gasp.

She knew it was his instinct which like hers could sense what had not been obvious to anybody else.

He stood for a moment looking at her in the firelight, then he sat down on the mattress facing her and took her hand in his.

"You look very beautiful!" he said softly. "I always wondered how long your hair was."

She felt herself blush and her eyes fell before his as she said:

"It is. . .wrong for you to. . .be here."

"It is never wrong for us to be together," he continued,

"and I could not sleep. When I felt you calling to me, my heart responded to your heart."

Pepita looked at him beseechingly and now he saw the traces of tears on her cheeks.

Very gently, as if he was afraid to frighten her, he bent forward and his lips were on hers.

He kissed her tenderly, as if she was very precious, and because it was different from any way in which he had kissed her before, she felt the tears fill her eyes, then run down her cheeks.

Now she was not crying because she was frightened.

Then he kissed her until her heart began to beat in a way that was only too familiar, and as Torquil's kisses became more insistent, more demanding, she felt as if he brought life back into her body with a rapture that was as if he carried her up to the stars.

When finally he raised his head, she was no longer feeling weak and helpless, but glowing with the wonder that he had evoked in her and pulsating with the ecstasy his kisses always gave her and which made her feel as if she were flying in the air and the earth was left far behind.

"I love you!" Torquil said in his deep voice. "It is so wonderful, my darling! I feel sensations I never knew existed, and when I kiss you I know that we belong to each other and that neither of us can ever be complete unless we are together."

"I. . .I. . .love you!" Pepita replied. "But you know it. . .is. . .wrong."

"It is right!" Torquil said fiercely. "Nothing could be more right than the love we have for each other, which is perfect and so much a part of our existence that we cannot live without it."

Then, as if he was afraid she would argue with him, he was kissing her again, kissing her until she felt as if there were a fire burning through her to reach out towards the fire that she felt on his lips.

Only when he released her mouth and kissed the softness of her neck did she feel a strange, wild emotion rise within her that she had never known before.

Then she made a little murmur of protest and tried to push him away from her.

At the same time her breath was coming in little gasps, her eyes felt heavy, and she wanted his kisses more than she had ever wanted anything in her whole life.

"I will not frighten you, my precious," Torquil said, and his voice was deep and a little hoarse. "I have so much to teach you that I cannot wait very much longer for us to be alone together and I can do so."

Pepita wanted to reply that it was something which would never happen because she must leave him.

But she knew for the moment she could not spoil the happiness of being with him and the wonder of his kisses, or take away the love she could see in his eyes.

"You are so beautiful," Torquil said, "but that is not the only reason why I love you. I adore your laughter, your clever little mind, the way you are always thinking of other people rather than yourself. I do not believe any woman could be more unselfish or more feminine."

He kissed her again, then raised her hand to his lips.

"All I want to do is to stay here all night kissing you and making love to you, but, my darling, I must let you sleep. You have been through a terrible traumatic experience today, and I want you to promise me that you will rest tomorrow."

"R-rest?" Pepita asked, hardly aware of what she was saying.

"The house will be filled with mourners," Torquil explained, "the blinds will be drawn, and it will all be very gloomy and unpleasant. I do not want you to be a part of it."

He put his hand on hers as he added:

"Stay here with the children, and I will come sometime during the day to take them for a walk. Naturally sport or anything like that will be taboo until after the Funeral."

"Y-yes. . .of course," Pepita murmured.

"When that is over, you and I will make plans," Torquil said. "All I want you to remember at the moment is that I love you, and that soon, very soon I will be able to prove to you how much!"

As if the idea excited him, he bent forward once again and kissed her until the flames flickered wildly in them both and Pepita wanted to be close and ever closer to him.

Then as if he forced himself to leave her he said:

"I adore you and no-one could be more wonderful! Dream of me, my precious one, as I shall be dreaming of you."

Then without waiting for her reply he went from the room, shutting the door very quietly behind him.

Chapter Seven

Pepita was saying good-night to Jeanie, who put her arms round her neck.

"I love you, Aunt Pepita!" she said. "And I love being here in this beautiful big Castle."

"You are happy, darling?" Pepita asked.

"Very, very happy!" Jeanie answered. "And tomorrow I am going to learn to dance a Reel!"

Pepita kissed her, then stood looking down at her as her eyes closed slowly, and she knew that by the time she left the bedroom Jeanie would be fast asleep.

She was saying good-bye to somebody who meant so much to her that she could hardly bear to think she would never see Jeanie again, at least until she was very much older.

She tried to put the thought from her as she went from Jeanie's room to Rory's, finding him sitting up in bed, reading a book.

"This is very interesting, Aunt Pepita," he said as she

came into the room. "It is all about the battles we have fought, and it mentions that my Clan was there and they fought very valiantly."

Pepita wanted to smile at the possessive note in his voice as he spoke of "my Clan," and she knew that already he was identifying himself with the McNairns.

The Duke had made it quite clear that in the years to come he would take over the Chieftainship.

As was usual in Scotland, only the men attended the Funeral of the Duchess, but Pepita had watched from the window as the cortège wended its way from the Castle towards the Ducal burial ground that was in the centre of one of the woods.

Rory was walking beside his grandfather immediately behind the coffin, and there was something in the sight of the two of them together that made the tears come into her eyes.

It was very obvious, however, that no-one in the Castle was really mourning the Duchess, despite the lowered blinds, crêpe veils, and black arm-bands.

Pepita, because she was English, felt she was an intruder and kept away from the hordes of relations of both Clans who came from all over Scotland, a great number of them having to stay in the Castle.

Now it was all over, the last guest having left after luncheon, and she knew that at dinner she and Torquil would be alone with the Duke.

'My last night,' she thought to herself, and felt an anguish that seemed to split her heart in two.

She went from Rory's room to her own, where Mrs. Sutherland was waiting for her.

"Everything's arranged, Miss," she said in a low voice as Pepita shut the door behind her. "One of my nephews'll carry yer trunks down to the Quay last thing, and a boat'll be waiting to row ye doon the coast at half-after-four in the morn'."

She paused, then added:

"The ship that'll carry ye to Edinburgh'll be leaving at five o'clock, an' ye mustna be late fer it."

"I will not be," Pepita answered, "and thank you for all you have done for me."

"I canna say it's been a pleasure," Mrs. Sutherland replied, "fer I've no wish tae see ye leave, but ye know yer ain mind, an' I'll no argue wi' ye."

"Thank you."

"I'll call ye at four o'clock," Mrs. Sutherland went on, "and I'll hae the money ready for ye then."

She looked to where Pepita's trunk was standing at the end of the room and added:

"I've packed everything for ye. All ye have tae do is to put in the gown ye'll be wearing for dinner. Yer travelling-suit and a warm coat which ye'll need are on the chair."

"Thank you. . .Mrs. Sutherland. . .thank you. . .very much indeed!"

It was difficult to say the words for fear she would burst into tears.

As if she understood what she was feeling, Mrs. Sutherland went from the room, saying as she did so:

"If ye want me tae fasten yer gown, ring the bell. I'll be in my ain room."

Pepita put her hands up to her face, fighting for composure, trying desperately to hold back the tears.

Now that the moment of leaving was actually upon her, she felt it impossible to do what she intended, and yet she knew there was no alternative.

She had to go, and to linger on would only make things worse.

The Tutor for Rory was arriving at the end of the week, and she had the suspicion that the very nice woman who had been engaged to teach both the children Reels was the Governess whom the Duke had in mind for Jeanie.

He had not said anything, but her instinct told her

that that was what he was planning, and she would not humiliate herself by waiting until he dismissed her.

She had not been alone with Torquil since he had come to her bedroom the night of the Duchess's death.

Yet she knew that he had been vividly aware of her, as she was of him, every time they were in the same room together.

Even though he was busy with all the arrangements for the Funeral and the mourners staying in the house, she was sure that he was thinking of her as she was thinking of him.

"I love him," she murmured now.

Although she might never see him again, he would always be in her heart.

Slowly she changed into the evening-gown that Mrs. Sutherland had left out for her.

She noticed vaguely that it had been her sister's and was almost too grand to wear for a quiet evening.

And yet she was glad that the last time Torquil saw her she would be looking her best.

With that thought in her mind, she took longer in arranging her hair than she usually did.

It was still too early to go to the Drawing-Room, and she opened the trunk to put in it the gown she had been wearing during the day.

As she did so there was a knock on the door, and she thought it must be Mrs. Sutherland coming to do up her gown.

"Come in!" she called, and added as the door opened: "Thank you for packing everything so beautifully, and far better than I could have done it myself!"

There was no answer, and Pepita turned her head, then saw that it was not Mrs. Sutherland but Torquil standing inside the room.

She gave an audible gasp as he walked forward a few paces before he said:

"Packing? What do you mean—you are packing?"

He was holding something in his hands, which he set down on a table at the bottom of the bed, then came towards her with his eyes on her trunk.

"What is happening? What are you doing?"

The questions were sharp and frightening.

"I. . .I am. . .going. . .away."

Pepita's voice was little above a whisper, and because she thought Torquil was angry she was trembling.

"Going away?" he repeated. "How can you do anything so cruel, so damnably cruel as to leave me?"

"I. . .I have to," Pepita argued. "Oh, darling. . .try to understand. . .I have to leave!"

"Why?"

"Because I. . .love you too much to. . .ruin your life."

It was difficult to say the words, and they were almost incoherent.

Then once again she gasped as Torquil put out his hands to hold her by the arms.

His fingers dug into her flesh, and when she looked at him she saw an expression of anger on his face that she had never seen before.

"How dare you!" he exclaimed. "How dare you go away! Do you not realise that wherever you went I would follow you, and however skilfully you tried to hide I would find you?"

The words were harsh and raw, and she knew he was angry because she had made him frightened that he might lose her.

"Please. . .understand," she pleaded. "Please realise that I cannot stay here and. . .destroy everything that is. . .familiar to you."

She gave a sob as she added:

"You would be. . .sent away as Alistair was. You would be. . .exiled, and I could not. . .bear that to happen to you."

"Why could you not bear it?"

She thought it was a strange question, but she answered:

"Because. . .I love you. . .I love you so much that I want to protect you."

"And you think you would be doing that by taking from me what matters more to me than life itself?"

He looked at her, then suddenly the anger was gone from his eyes.

As he pulled her almost roughly closer to him, his expression was very tender.

"What does anything matter, my foolish one," he asked, "except our love? We have something which is far more important than position, family, Clan, or nationality."

Pepita had hidden her face against him while he was speaking, and now he put his fingers under her chin and turned her face up to his.

She was very pale and the tears were running down her cheeks.

He looked at her for a long moment before he said fiercely:

"You are mine, and neither man nor God shall take you from me!"

Then his lips were on hers, and for a moment they were hard and hurt the softness of her mouth, until because they were touching each other the rapture of it rose in both of them.

Now his lips became more demanding, more possessive, and no longer hurt her.

He drew her closer and still closer and kissed her until once again she was part of him and they were indivisible.

She felt herself quiver with a rapture that was inescapable, and when finally he raised his head she could only whisper brokenly:

"I love you. . .I love you!"

Once again she hid her face against his neck.

"You will never leave me!" Torquil said, and she thought as he spoke that his voice was unsteady too.

She felt his lips on her hair as he went on:

"We are going to be married immediately, and I came here to tell you that we would discuss it with the Duke tonight."

"No. . .no!" Pepita cried in terror.

She looked up at him as she spoke and was surprised to see that he was smiling and there was an unmistakable look of happiness in his eyes.

"You have not asked me why I came to see you just now," he said quietly, "but it is a good thing I did!"

He glanced disparagingly at her open trunk, then as she was unable to speak he went on:

"Actually, I brought you a present!"

"A. . .present?" Pepita murmured.

"A somewhat unexpected one which needs a little explanation."

He did not move.

She was still close in his arms, but she looked to where he had set down what he had been carrying in his hands and saw that it was something wrapped up in white paper.

"First, my precious," Torquil said, "I want you to tell me the name of your grandmother."

"M-my. . .grandmother?" Pepita asked in astonishment.

"Your father's mother," Torquil persisted. "Do you remember her name?"

"Of course," Pepita replied, "but I never knew her because she died when my father was quite small and my grandfather married again. Papa often talked of his Stepmother, of whom he was very fond, but he could not remember his own mother."

"But you knew her name?"

138

"It was Lamont, and I always thought she must originally have been of French origin."

Torquil smiled.

"No, darling—Scottish!"

Pepita stared at him.

"What. . .are you saying?"

"I am telling you," Torquil answered, "what you should have found out a long time ago, that your grandmother, Mary Lamont, came from a Clan which was established in Cowal in the middle of the Thirteenth Century."

Pepita stared at him as if spellbound, and he went on:

"The Lamonts still own land in Cowal and there are a great number of the Clan living round Loch Striven."

There was silence before Pepita said:

"I cannot. . .believe that what you are. . .telling me is. . .true!"

"What I am telling you," Torquil said, "is that you are in fact one-quarter Scottish on your father's side, and your mother some way back had a great-great-grandparent who was a Rose."

"Rose?" Pepita questioned. "Surely that is not a Scottish name?"

Torquil laughed.

"The Roses settled in the district of Nairn in the Twelfth Century, and one of them, a great-grandparent of yours, received 'Bonnie Prince Charlie' at Kilravock just before Culloden."

"How can this. . .possibly be. . .true?" Pepita gasped.

"I see, my precious, that you are very ignorant about your ancestors. You need a Scottish Tutor, and I offer myself as a very competent teacher on the subject as well as on others."

She knew he was teasing her, but because what he had just told her was so overwhelming, she could only hide her tears against him.

Now they were tears of relief, even though what he had said still seemed incredible.

As if he understood what she was feeling, Torquil continued:

"I could not believe that in any distinguished family like that of your father there would not be one Scottish ancestor. So I sent somebody I trusted and who is very knowledgeable on Genealogy to the College of Arms in Edinburgh."

He kissed her forehead before he went on:

"He returned this evening with the information that after all your heart-burning you have enough Scottish blood in you, my darling, to make you, from the Duke's and everybody else's point of view, a very suitable wife for one of the McNairns."

"I. . .I cannot. . .believe it!" Pepita cried. "I thought I had to. . .leave you. . .but now I can. . .stay?"

It was a question and very gently Torquil turned her face up to his again.

"Do you really think I could ever let you go?" he asked. "You are part of me, and without you I have no wish to go on living."

Pepita put her arms round his neck and drew his head down to hers.

"How can you have been so. . .clever as to. . .discover all this? But because you have. . .I am the happiest person in the. . .world!"

Even so she could not stop her tears from falling, and gently Torquil wiped them away before he said:

"You will never be unhappy again. We have so much to do together here, and, my darling, although you and I will help look after Rory and Jeanie, I want a family of my own."

"That is. . .what I want to. . .give you," Pepita whispered.

Because she felt shy, she pressed her cheek against his.

"Now that is settled!" Torquil said in a different tone of voice. "You can now unpack your trunk, although it will be only a few days before we are married and I take you to my own Castle for our honeymoon."

"Can we. . .really do. . .that?"

He smiled at her.

"I think we both know that the Duke will look after the children and you need not worry about them. Personally, I think it is time you looked after me!"

"That is. . .what I was. . .trying to do."

"Let me make this quite clear," Torquil said. "You will never leave me again or even think of doing so! You are mine, and I shall be jealous if you ever think of anything else except me."

He pulled her closer to him and kissed her passionately and demandingly.

It was impossible to tell him that she was his completely, but she was aware that he knew it already.

*   *   *

Both Torquil and Pepita were smiling as they walked hand-in-hand down the corridor to the Drawing-Room.

The Duke was waiting for them and there was a slight frown between his eyes because they were late.

Then as they walked in through the Drawing-Room door, his eyes were on Pepita, and as she and Torquil came towards him he asked with a note of astonishment in his voice:

"Why are you wearing a plaid of the Lamonts?"

It was the present that Torquil had bought Pepita, a plaid made of her grandmother's tartan.

He had arranged it in the correct fashion on her shoulders, fastening it with a magnificent silver brooch with a huge amethyst in the centre of it.

Now as she stood in front of the Duke and saw the

plexity in his eyes, she wanted to laugh, but Torquil
swered the question for her.

"It is the tartan to which she is entitled!"

"Entitled?" the Duke questioned.

"Pepita's grandmother was the daughter of the Laird
of Striven."

The Duke looked astonished.

"Are you sure?"

In answer Torquil drew from his breast-pocket the
letter which had been brought from Edinburgh.

It was signed by the Lord Lyon and declared that
after very minor investigations—and there were a great
many more the College could do—it had been found that
Sir Robert Linford's mother was Mary Lamont.

In a postscript the Lord Lyon had added that Sir
Robert's wife, Elizabeth Sheringham, had a distant ancestor by the name of Hugh Rose of Kilravock.

"Why was I not told this before?" the Duke asked
angrily as he finished reading the letter.

Instinctively Pepita knew he was thinking that had he
been aware that her sister was one-quarter Scottish, as she
was, he would have accepted her as Alistair's wife.

Then there would have been no reason for him to
exile his son and cut him out of his life.

Because she felt how sad it was for the Duke, Pepita
impulsively put out her hand and laid it on his arm.

"I am sorry," she said, and knew he understood to
what she was referring.

After a little pause she went on:

"My father was never very interested in his ante-
cedents, and I think that is true of most English people,
unless they come from one of the great ancestral families.
It is the Scots to whom breeding and blood means so
much. And now I am very. . .proud indeed to know that
I. . .belong to the. . .Lamont Clan!"

She spoke a little tentatively in case the Duke should

think she was being presumptuous, but there was only a slight silence before he said:

"It must have been your great-uncle who was a close friend of mine, when we were young. I will inform him who you are, and tell him that my grandchildren are related to him."

"He will be delighted!" Torquil said. "After all, the Duke of Strathnairn is a very important personality in Scotland."

Pepita was half-afraid that the Duke might be annoyed at the way in which Torquil was teasing him, which was the way he teased her.

Instead, the Duke replied:

"I am delighted you think so. It was clever of you, Torquil, to discover what should have come to light long ago."

"It is particularly important to me," Torquil replied, "because Pepita has promised to marry me, and I hope, Sir, you will give us your blessing."

Pepita held her breath, but the Duke, instead of looking angry, as she had feared he might, merely smiled.

"I am not surprised," he said, "and I suppose that you will wish me to give the bride away?"

"Of course!" Torquil answered. "What could be more appropriate?"

The Duke looked at Pepita and said:

"I might have guessed, when you were so brave that you were one of us. Welcome, Pepita Linford, to my family!"

He held out his hand as he spoke, and because she had seen how he was approached by his Clansmen, she went down on one knee and kissed his hand.

* * *

Pepita stood at the window and looked at the morning mist over the sea.

She and Torquil had been married very quietly because the Duke was in deep mourning, but Torquil would not wait until they could have a grand wedding.

Pepita actually was very thankful that she did not have to face too many people all at once.

She had always wanted a wedding like her sister's, where she could concentrate on the man she loved and not have to think about anyone else.

They had therefore all gone together to the Kirk, which was decorated on Torquil's instructions with masses of white heather.

There they were married, not by the Minister who had preached so violently against the Clearances but by a McNairn who was a Canon at Edinburgh Cathedral.

Rory had carried her train up the aisle and Jeanie was her only bridesmaid.

To Pepita the small building seemed filled with the voices of angels, and she felt that Denise and Alistair were very close to her and glad at what was happening.

In the Ducal pew there was one member of her own family, and that was the Laird of the Clan Lamont, who came from Loch Striven at the Duke's invitation.

He was a handsome man, very distinguished in his green and blue kilt, and Pepita felt proud to belong to him.

When she thought about it she could not help asking herself how she and Denise had been so stupid as not to have found out that there had been Scots in their family in the past.

But she was very young when Denise had married, and it had never crossed their minds that things might have been very different if they had not been branded so contemptuously by the Duke as Sassenachs.

Torquil had said that he would never lose her, and she knew he was speaking the truth when he had said he would have followed her wherever she went.

Yet, she knew she would always have felt guilty, now that she had seen what Scotland was like, in taking him away from his native land.

Looking back, she could remember moments when she had thought her brother-in-law was thinking wistfully of his home and his own people.

Nevertheless, because he was by nature happy-go-lucky and not in the least introspective, she was certain that he spoke the truth when he said that his happiness with her sister made it impossible for him to have any regrets or to think for a moment of what he had lost.

Now, although it seemed incredible, where she was concerned a Fairy Godmother in the shape of the College of Arms in Edinburgh had changed everything.

To the Scots she was a Scot, and although Torquil had said that once she was his wife he would never allow her to wear anything but his tartan, she knew that the Lamont plaid he had given her would always be something very special.

She would keep and treasure it, and it would mean far more to her than any jewel, however valuable.

When Torquil had put the ring on her finger and she realised she was his wife, she felt as if a Divine Light from Heaven itself shone over them.

She thanked God that her prayers had been answered, and now the future was very different from what she had feared it would be.

The night before her wedding she had prayed that she would make Torquil a good wife and make him happy forever.

Then she said prayers of thankfulness that she was not sailing away to the South to an unknown future of privation and poverty, where she would have to hide in case Torquil should find her.

"How can I be grateful enough, God?" she asked.

She knew that somehow she would try to pay back

what she had received by helping those who were not so fortunate as she was.

When they were driving back from the Kirk, Torquil had taken her hand in his and kissed first her wedding-ring, then each finger, one by one, until finally his lips rested in her palm.

There was no need for words, because his lips said it for him.

Then as they turned into the long drive which led to the Castle, they heard the music of the bagpipes.

As she listened, Pepita felt something within her leap towards them and knew that now the music could mean more to her than she had ever allowed it to do before.

When she had heard the pipes first on the night when the Piper had played round the table at dinner, she had thought that they lifted her heart in a strange way and felt almost as if the music spoke to her.

At the same time, she thought she was being imaginative.

Now she knew it was what all Scots feel when they hear the music that is peculiarly their own.

It led them into battle, and it gave expression to their feelings, whether they were glad or sad, happy or miserable.

The pipes expressed what could not be said in words, because they spoke from the heart, and that is what every Scot hears and to which he responds with his very soul.

At the small Reception in the Castle, after having cut and eaten the wedding-cake that had been baked, Pepita thought, with love, the Duke had toasted them with a sincerity that made her very happy, and they finally drove away along the coast-road which led to Torquil's Castle.

It was when she had a last glimpse of Rory and Jeanie waving to them from the doorstep that Pepita really understood that she was starting out on a new life of her own with the man she loved.

As if he knew what she was feeling, Torquil, who was

driving two spirited horses that Pepita had not seen before, looked down at her.

"This is where our life together begins," he said, "and I vow that I will make you happy."

"I am happy, darling," she answered, "and so excited that it is. . .impossible to put it into. . .words!"

He drew in his breath before he said:

"You can tell me about it, without words, when we reach home."

She saw the fire in his eyes as he spoke, then as he turned again to his horses, she blushed and pressed her cheek against his shoulder.

* * *

It had been a rough night, but now the rising sun was turning the water to gold and casting strange lights on the moors.

There was still a little of the sable of the night left and the last star was fading away into space.

It was so beautiful that Pepita felt as if she had stepped into a magical world which had always been part of her dreams.

Then as she stood there thinking that it was not only the dawn of a new day but the dawn of a new life, she heard Torquil's voice ask:

"Why have you left me?"

"I am looking at the dawn, darling," she replied. "I feel it is symbolic of what is happening to us."

"I am lonely without you," he replied. "Come here!"

There was an unmistakable command in his words, and Pepita turned to smile at him before she looked back once again at the dazzling beauty of the sea.

Then, because not even the most breath-taking view she had ever seen could be as alluring as her husband, she ran back to the great carved and canopied bed.

In it Torquil's ancestors had been born and died and always another generation had arrived to carry on the name.

His arms went out to pull her closer to him, and as her head seemed to fall naturally against his shoulder, she whispered:

"Is it true. . .really true that I am here and we are. . .married and I need never be afraid or alone again?"

"It is true, my darling one," Torquil said, "and like you I feel it is a dream come true. At the same time, we have fought against immeasurable odds to be with each other, and won!"

The note of triumph in his voice was unmistakable, and Pepita gave a little laugh as she said:

"*You* won! I admit I was weak and faint-hearted, but only because I loved you!"

"I know that, my precious one," he said, "but you did not realise that as far as I was concerned I was prepared to lose the whole world and my hope of Heaven to gain you."

"How can you be so wonderful?" Pepita asked. "Last night, darling, you made me. . .realise that we are. . .one person, and it is. . .impossible for us not to be. . .together."

"I made you happy, and I did not frighten you?" Torquil asked quickly.

"I could never be frightened of. . .you."

He drew her closer to him, and now his hand was touching her body, and his lips were against the softness of her cheeks.

"How can you be so different from anybody else I have ever known?" he asked. "How can you excite me to madness as a woman, and yet at the same time I want to worship you because you are so pure and perfect that I feel you are not really human?"

"I am very human. . .my darling. . .when you. . .kiss me," Pepita whispered, "and the only thing that makes me. . .afraid now is that we are. . .too happy, and at any moment the Vikings might attack us. . .or the McDonavans come creeping over the moors to fight us."

Torquil laughed before he replied:

"Thank God, nothing like that can happen today, but there are always problems, always difficulties, and always suffering in Scotland. What you have to do, my sweet, is to help me to look after those who cannot look after themselves."

"You know I will do. . .anything you. . .want me to. . .do," Pepita said, "but firstly you have so much to teach me about this country of which I am now a part, and you must prevent me as a. . .Sassenach from making any. . .mistakes."

"You are never to call yourself that again!" Torquil said sharply. "You are not a Sassenach! You have Lamont blood in your veins and you are also my wife! You can forget everything that is English and concentrate on the glory that burns in us both because we can say proudly that we are Scots."

Pepita heard the pride in his voice, and she thought how much she had suffered, thinking that as she was English she was an outcast.

She had been afraid of the Duke sending her away from the children, and she remembered how the Duchess's hatred had vibrated towards her so that she could not escape from it.

She was ashamed now that she had been so weak and so fearful.

Her Scottish ancestors had fought against incredible odds to survive the misery of being conquered by the English. Their spirit had remained undefeated and gradually they had won back all they had lost.

It was not their physical strength that had made them succeed, but the spirit within them which nothing could extinguish.

It was that spirit that she and Torquil must give to their children and they in their turn to their children.

It was a spirit which nothing could destroy and which would never die.

These thoughts all flashed through her mind, then she was aware that Torquil was touching her and his lips were moving over the softness of her skin.

Now the fire that was never far from the surface was flickering like little flames within her body, awakened by the raging fire that was in his heart and on his lips.

"I love. . .you!" she whispered.

As if the softness of her words made the flames leap higher and higher, she heard the passion in his voice as he replied:

"I adore you! You are mine! Give me yourself and your love, for I cannot live without them."

"They are. . .yours," Pepita answered. "Yours, completely and. . .absolutely. Oh, darling Torquil, love me. . .I want you to. . .love me!"

Then as his lips held her captive and his heart was beating on hers, he carried her up into the sky, and as he made her his, she knew their love was eternal.

Outside the Castle, the sun rose over the shimmering sea, turning the lights on the moors from purple to gold as the wind mingled the scent of the heather and peat with the salt of the sea.

It was the haunting scent of Scotland, which is part of its magic and goes with Scots wherever they travel and which they can never forget.

ABOUT THE AUTHOR

BARBARA CARTLAND, the world's most famous romantic novelist, who is also an historian, playwright, lecturer, political speaker and television personality, has now written over 350 books and sold over 350 million books throughout the world.

She has also had many historical works published and has written four autobiographies as well as the biographies of her mother and that of her brother, Ronald Cartland, who was the first Member of Parliament to be killed in World War II. This book has a preface by Sir Winston Churchill and has just been republished with an introduction by Sir Arthur Bryant.

Love at the Helm, a novel written with the help and inspiration of the late Earl Mountbatten of Burma, Uncle of His Royal Highness Prince Philip, is being sold for the Mountbatten Memorial Trust.

In 1978, Miss Cartland sang an Album of Love Songs with the Royal Philharmonic Orchestra.

In 1976, by writing twenty-one books, she broke the world record and has continued for the following six years with 24, 20, 23, 24, 24, and 25. She is in the *Guinness Book of World Records* as currently the top-selling authoress in the world.

She is unique in that she was #1 and #2 in the Dalton List of BestSellers, and one week had four books in the top twenty.

In private life Barbara Cartland, who is a Dame of the Order of St. John of Jerusalem, Chairman of the St. John Council in Hertfordshire and Deputy President of the St. John Ambulance Brigade, has also fought for better conditions and salaries for midwives and nurses.

Barbara Cartland is deeply interested in vitamin therapy and is President of the British National Association for Health. Her book, *The Magic of Honey*, has sold throughout the world and is translated into many languages.

Her designs, *Decorating with Love*, are being sold all over the USA and the National Home Fashions League made her "Woman of Achievement" in 1981.

Barbara Cartland Romances (book of cartoons) has just been published in Great Britain and the United States, and several countries in Europe carry the strip cartoons of her novels.